AND THEIR *Lives Were* CHANGED

AND THEIR *Lives Were* CHANGED

M. J. FERGUSON

TATE PUBLISHING
AND ENTERPRISES, LLC

And Their Lives Were Changed

This novel is a work of fiction. However, several names, descriptions, entities, and incidents included in the story are based on the lives of real people.

The opinions expressed by the author are not necessarily those of Tate Publishing, LLC.

Published by Tate Publishing & Enterprises, LLC
127 E. Trade Center Terrace | Mustang, Oklahoma 73064 USA
1.888.361.9473 | www.tatepublishing.com

Tate Publishing is committed to excellence in the publishing industry. The company reflects the philosophy established by the founders, based on Psalm 68:11,
"The Lord gave the word and great was the company of those who published it."

Cover design by Norlan Balazo
Interior design by Richell Balansag

Published in the United States of America

ISBN: 978-1-68319-087-5
1. Fiction / Christian / General
2. Fiction / Christian / Historical
16.07.21

And Their Lives Were Changed

Contents

Preface

While Jesus was on this earth, many people had personal contact with Him. Walking, talking, eating, living, and observing. Some were healed, some were forgiven, some were friends, many were witnesses to His interactions with the multitudes. Everyone was "touched" in a personal or unique way. Some with love and appreciation, and some with resistance and resentment.

This book takes you into the *possible* thoughts, words, and actions of seventeen different individuals who had personal contact with Jesus Christ while he was living among His people. Some characters were mentioned in the Bible only briefly, and some were not even given names. In order to *tell* their stories, I have added names and some possible backgrounds. Occasionally, scenarios and events (not stated in Holy Scripture) were taken from various historians. In no place is there a *contradiction* to the Bible.

Each chapter is "the telling" of his or her own story. At the end of their story, they tell you, the reader, how their lives were changed.

Joseph

Joseph (The Broken)

My life began and ended on the same day—the day my beautiful and beloved wife, Anna, died.

Anna and I had known each other most of our lives and were married for about fourteen years. I was born just south of Jerusalem and Anna here in Nazareth. Since both of us were raised in this village, she was my childhood sweetheart. Our parents finally agreed (after much pleading—mostly on my part) that we could marry since I had a small, but growing carpentry shop. Her father said, "At least he *looks* like he might have potential." (Anna's father was a good man, an honest man, but he always intimidated me.) I realized I needed to work hard to give Anna the comfortable home I had promised her *and* her papa.

Anna was a creative cook with vegetables and herbs that came mostly from her own garden. The delicious meals she prepared added a few unwelcome inches to my waist. Many in our community admired her, and her parents appeared pleased—even with *me!* We eventually had a wonderful family with three beautiful and extremely active boys.

Anna's fourth pregnancy seemed different and difficult from the start. She appeared more tired and a bit weaker than her previous three pregnancies. As I think back, I had often thought, *Is she struggling to keep up with our energetic boys and all that is expected for their care? Am I presuming and expecting too much? Am I not helping as I should?* All those questions and more went through my spinning mind.

Anna's delivery was long and difficult. At first, I was not allowed in the room with Anna and Sara, the midwife. Eventually, however, Sara called me in to give strength and encouragement to my wife. Finally, our baby was born. Sara worked hard and skillfully, but could not stop the bleeding—the hemorrhaging! So much blood! Then tragedy struck. Unspeakable tragedy! The baby was crying, but Anna was silent. Silent! *Forever silent!*

Brokenhearted, I held her lifeless body close to my breast. Rocking back and forth. Rocking for comfort. Rocking for her. Rocking for me. Rocking and rocking. Crying, I whispered, "I love you so much. What am I going to do without you? What will our boys and the new baby do without you? How can I possibly take care of a newborn baby?"

Sara held our newly-born infant while standing in the doorway, sobbing, dabbing her eyes, and wiping her nose with her apron. She seemed unsure of how to give comfort for this tragedy. It was much too early, anyway, for comfort. She just gave me privacy and distance—something I appreciated, but was unable to express.

Eventually, Sara ushered in our boys who were puzzled about my crying. The two younger boys were confused, but James seemed to understand and revealed his deep despair by kneeling beside his mother and me with tears running down his cheeks. I was unable to explain what had happened because I didn't know how. Why? *Why?* But Sara, bless her heart, did her best to console and ease their young, questioning, and hurting hearts.

Finally, after what seemed an eternity and yet too soon, Anna was taken from me. Too weak to follow, I stayed on my knees beside our empty bed for the rest of the night.

The next morning, with my eyes still swollen and red, I looked for Sara. I needn't have worried. She had taken charge of my household during the night by putting the boys to bed and giving them something to eat in the morning. She also found a way to feed the baby! *Oh, the baby! What about the baby? Do I now have four sons or...or is it a girl? Do I have a daughter?* Yes! I have a daughter, a beautiful daughter, and I will name her after her mother, Anna.

My grief was overwhelming! Grief and despair came from everywhere—the walls, the furniture, *the empty bed!* Grief came even from those who arrived to comfort.

As evening approached again, and as difficult as it was, I understood I needed to get control of myself and make some realistic plans. Plans that would hold my family together, or at least keep us from falling apart. Deep despair! I needed plans that would make sense and give my children and me some order and direction. Plans for the future. Plans and reasons to continue to live!

Sara was a short, plump widow who had ebony eyes and unruly gray hair. She lived a few doors down the lane from us. Her husband had died several years ago, leaving her without any support except for her sons who lived nearby. But, being a very resourceful woman, she found ways to earn a little extra money. She had been a midwife and babysitter to those in our village for many years. She raised six children of her own. Sara was a self-proclaimed Auntie or Grandmama to most of the town's children. Thankfully, Sara was here every day and kept our house in order and watched over my children while I was working—and grieving.

One day, after a few weeks, I asked, "Sara, would you consider moving into my house with the boys and me and sleeping in my bed?" Her eyebrows shot up and she gasped as she put her plump hand over her mouth.

Horrified, I suddenly realized what an inappropriate request I had made—or at least what it *sounded* like. "No, no, no, Sara, please forgive me! I am just asking that you be here *all* the time for my children and raise them as your own. I will make a bed for myself in my workshop. We could not have come this far without you. The boys and baby Anna love you. And we would be honored and blessed to have you staying with us. I cannot afford to pay a lot of money, but I will pay what I can. Will you please consider this? Please?"

Realizing I had spilled my request so rapidly, I was afraid it was all too much for her to understand the sincerity of my need. So all I added was, "Please, Sara. Will you seriously consider my request?"

Sara closed her eyes, let out a long breath, and began to laugh with one hand still covering her mouth, the other hand on her rotund abdomen. "Joseph," she finally said, "you know I love you as one of my own sons, and your sons as my grandsons. And, of course, your precious baby, Anna! Yes, *I* would be the honored one. Tomorrow, I'll ask one of my own sons to help me move."

So that is how Widow Sara came to live with my children and me. She was always cheerful. She taught and corrected my sons with tenderness.

Her cooking was not as tasty or creative as my Anna's, but there was always plenty of it. Her wonderful bread, however, was the envy of the village women. We were tremendously blessed having such a loving woman in our home and taking care of *us*.

One day, about a year and a half after Anna's death, Sara announced, "Joseph, I think it is time you found a wife for yourself and a mother for your children. You know, I am not getting any younger. I cannot stay with you until your children are grown. I'll be too old!"

Those words from Sara sent a hot jolt down my spine that almost buckled my knees. Things were going just fine the way they were; but, yes, I realized Sara was getting up in her years. She *was* too old to be raising another family! I didn't know what to say, so I just pretended I didn't hear her, and continued working on the cabinet I was making. Sara didn't say anything more, but I knew she wouldn't let it *drop!* She just turned and walked back into the house.

Sara knew everyone in our village and was respected and loved by most. She had rosy cheeks, dancing ebony eyes, and could talk the fleece off the sheep. And that's how Sara became the new self-proclaimed matchmaker of Nazareth.

A couple of days later, while at the dinner table, it came! Again! The *talk* I was dreading—words from the matchmaker.

"Joseph!" (I didn't look up.) "Joseph," she said a little louder. "I have found a wife for you—a perfect match. She is quite young and a little too skinny for my taste, but she is a good girl, a sweet girl, and she will make a good wife and mother. She comes from a poor but respected family. Her name is Mary. Perhaps you have seen her?"

"No, I don't know who you are talking about, and *no*, I am *not* interested!" I said firmly but cautiously.

"Joseph, please! Mary is the perfect match for you. I understand she is quite young and may be only ten or so years older than James, your eldest. I have checked around and apparently she hasn't learned to cook, but she is very skilled in making baskets, and keeps a beautiful garden for her parents. As for her cooking, she's young and can *learn!*" It seemed that all this was said without Sara taking a breath. Then she added, "I'll just *casually* bring her by your workshop tomorrow."

Oh, great! I thought sarcastically. *That is just great!*

I knew Sara was right about finding a mother for my children. But, a *wife* for me? I was not interested and I told her so—very *carefully*, you understand. Sara could easily put me in my corner with a look from her raven-black eyes!

True to her word, Sara "casually" brought Mary by my workshop. She was correct in her description of the girl. Mary looked young, even younger than her years. Stifling a laugh to myself, I thought, *She is just a child! Is this child for me or for my son?* Yes, she was very thin—even skinny! But she had a captivating aura of innocence and purity about her. We both said our polite greetings then she was gone. I could still hear Sara talking as they rounded the corner outside my workshop.

I went back to my work, but I couldn't get Mary out of my mind. Maybe, just *maybe*, I would keep my eye out for a chance to see her again. "This is ridiculous!" I said aloud, but softly. "Why would she be interested in marrying a man of my age—and a widower with *four* children?" But I found myself humming a simple melody the rest of the day. And the hammer injury to my thumb didn't hurt as much anymore!

At the evening meal that night, all was quiet until Sara said, "Well?"

"Well, what?"

"Joseph, you know very well *what*! What do you think of Mary? Isn't she sweet? I think you should make something special for her. Construct a little *something* from your workshop, something by your own hands. I think she would like that."

And, that's how my *new* life began! In the evenings during my downtime, I carved a little donkey pulling a cart. Even if I say so myself, it was attractive and I was pleased with it and hoped Mary would like it too.

Another week passed. Nervously, I walked up to her while she was pulling vegetables from her garden. I took my gift out of the pocket of my work apron and stammered something like, "Hello, Mary. I just carved this little donkey and cart and thought you might like to have it." She seemed so surprised, but pleased. She turned it over and over in her dirty, but small, petite hands. We had a short but pleasant chat. A chat about nothing—the weather, her garden, and the sheep grazing on the hillside. You know, nothing important! She thanked me again. I said an awkward good-bye and left.

Yes, I was beginning to think a lot about Mary, and she seemed to enjoy my company too when we "accidentally" met in the village. *Is this a possibility—her being my wife and a mother to my children?*

It took a lot of courage, but at Sara's persistent nagging (the nagging I had grown to expect, *but not appreciate),* I went to see Mary's father to ask permission for her hand in marriage. As I approached the door, I quickly checked *(again)* to see if all the sawdust and wood shavings had been brushed off my clothes and out of my hair and beard. I came with my "basket" loaded to impress him. Loaded with reasons. Loaded with promises. I must admit, my *reasons* were a little weak, but I felt my *promises* were strong—as strong as I could make them. I laid all my reasons and *promises* at Papa's feet.

Mary's father sat for a long time, just looking at me. No smile, no frown. It was like he didn't even acknowledge my being there, right in front of him! *Oh no!* A thousand thoughts raced through my head. *What is he going to do now? What will he do with me? What will he do* to *me! Is he going to throw me out of his house?* I guess I couldn't really blame him, but over the last few months, I had grown to admire and have great affection for Mary. Yes, I even wanted to marry her!

Finally, with the silence nearly deafening, he said, "Fine." He stood, I stood. He then gave me a business-like embrace, turned, and walked out of the room.

Fine? Fine? With my head spinning, my face red, and sweat running down the middle of my back, I asked myself, *What just happened here? Did I get permission to marry his daughter or not? What does "fine" mean? Can I now go to Mary and propose to her? Do I sit back down? Is Mary's papa coming back?*

After a few moments, I felt it best to leave with what dignity I could feign. I opened the door, looked around the room several times, walked out, and closed the door behind me. I just stood outside awhile, trying to collect some strength in my legs. Before I got all the way home, however, my legs felt like dancing with my feet barely touching the ground. My heart began to lighten. I felt like my head was in the clouds. *Yes! Yes, I was given permission—I think. In a few days, after I conjure up more courage, I'll go to Mary.*

Again, with my "basket" reloaded with promises, I made plans to talk to Mary about my heart's desire. *I hope she will say, "Yes." Or at least, "Let me think about it."*

Has my life changed? Yes, I would have to admit many things in my life have changed over the past couple of years—sadly, not all for the better. But I had the feeling my life was about to have many more changes. I pray there will be good changes for my children and me and, of course, for Mary.

Mary (The Innocent)

"Mary," I heard my father calling me. I was in the garden, pulling weeds, picking a few vegetables, and putting them in one of my older baskets. "Yes, Papa, I'll be right there," I answered. "Let me wash my hands first." I walked into the cool house, thankful to be getting out of the hot sun.

"I have something important to tell to you." This sounded serious, so I pulled up a stool to sit on. I sat close to Papa's knees while he sat in his big Papa's Chair. He seemed at a loss for words and a bit uneasy, which was very unusual for him. Papa was always strong and confident. Eventually, after looking around the room, like searching for special words, he broke into a big grin and said, "Mary."

"Yes, Papa, I am here. What is it?"

"Mary." Again a pensive pause. I thought it best not to press him, so I sat very still, looking into his kind eyes. His smile faded, and I felt apprehensive. I knew it had something to do with me, but what? What could be so important to cause this obvious anxiety in my papa—my secured and assured papa!

"Mary, you know I love you."

"Yes, of course, Papa, and I love you!"

"Well, um, um—" His words now began to flow rapidly, "A proposal of marriage has been requested, and I have given my permission for you to marry—marry Joseph…Joseph the carpenter." Then adding quickly, "He is a good man, an honest man, a hard worker, and I expect he will provide well for you."

"What? But, Papa!" I couldn't believe my ears! "Joseph? Joseph the carpenter? Joseph, whose wife died a couple of years ago?" *How can Papa promise me to this man?* "I know he is a nice man, Papa, but *no*, Papa! Please! He is so old, and he has *four* children! How can I be a mother to his *four* children, especially when his oldest is nearly *my* age?" I put my hands on his knee—pleading with my hands, pleading with my tear-rimmed eyes. A plea I was hopeful, but doubtful, would change his mind. *How can he do this to me?*

"Don't exaggerate, Mary! There may be ten or more years' difference in age between you and James," he said with a little irritation in his usually soft-spoken voice. "So, my daughter, I have given Joseph my permission, and you *will* marry him!" My father had made his announcement and decision, and I was terrified that was the end of it! No more discussion, no more argument, no more pleading! I fought back the tears.

I got up from the stool that I was sitting on, weak in my knees, and sick to my stomach. I went back out to the garden to think, and *think!* My mind was whirling. *I know that arranged marriages are the custom of our people, but I am too young, and he is so old and with a family. A family of boys and a baby girl!*

Thinking back over the last couple of months, I wondered. *Is this possibly why Joseph seems to be paying special attention to me? He is always smiling when I catch him looking at me. The little gift of a small wooden hand-carved donkey, an occasional flower he "picked along the way," or a loaf of Sara's delicious bread. Sara took me to Joseph's workshop one day; is she behind all this? Is she the matchmaker? How can I be so blind—so naïve?*

Sara is living in Joseph's house and takes good care of his children. They don't need me! Joseph doesn't need me! Yes, he seems loving, kind, and attentive to his children, a good father. I like Joseph—but marry him? How can I? How can Papa promise me to Joseph? A thousand jumbled thoughts ran through my spinning head.

Suddenly a frightening consideration came to me—a *possible* way out. I ran back into the house, where Papa was still sitting in his chair. I cried, "But, Papa, I can't *cook!* I have never *learned* to cook! How can I feed a family when I can't cook?"

"I know, Mary. I know! You have always been such a sweet and tenderhearted child. Sometimes your head is in the clouds or soaring toward the stars. Sometimes it seems you would rather be flying as free as the birds or bouncing in the garden with the butterflies. Perhaps your mama and I have been neglectful in preparing you for your future. So now, Mary, we will need to work on the more practical aspects of your life of being a wife and mother. Your mama and I will help you!"

Papa put his hands on my flushed cheeks and looked directly into my swollen and red eyes. "So when Joseph talks to you—and I am pretty sure he will—you will know this is my wish, my *plan* for you," he said tenderly, but firmly. *Do I see a pool of tears about to spill down Papa's cheeks too?*

"Yes, Papa," I whispered.

For the next couple of days, I tried to stay in the house as much as possible to avoid Joseph. It gave me more time to think. Think of Joseph. Think of his children. Think of being a wife and a *mother* so soon in my life! I must admit my heart began to soften to the idea, and I found myself being a little delighted. Pleased that he desired me. *Me!* Was this God's plan for my life? *Oh, there is so much for me to learn—like cooking! How can I ever learn to cook like my mother, or like Sara?* I closed my eyes and groaned softly to myself.

True to my papa's declaration and true to my anxiety, Joseph asked to talk to me one cool evening. We walked in my garden among the herbs and vegetables. I don't remember his exact words, as they seemed a bit halting and jumbled. But Joseph *finally* expressed his affection for me and his longing for our life together. He was not eloquent but *sincere*. He was not forceful but *genuine*. After listening to Joseph, I found myself wishing the same goals for our future and agreeing to be his wife. Besides, I had no choice! Papa had spoken!

After a couple of days, both of my parents accompanied Joseph and me to the synagogue. With a small bouquet of wildflowers in my hand, Joseph and I went to the priest to have our betrothal blessed. We would marry in one year!

There were lots of preparations to be done, along with learning to cook! Mama and Sara were so tolerant with me and did their best with my clumsy attempts. Mama used her special herbs for tasty meals, and Sara instructed for large proportions. Also, Sara patiently showed me how to make her celebrated bread. *How will I ever learn this?* But I soon found myself longing to be a good wife and mother and make Joseph and his children happy.

One day, while home alone, I was trying my unskilled hand at making bread. I had flour all over me, the table, the floor, and the sticky dough was hard to control. Sara made it look so easy! I knew I must look a fright and laughed to myself. Laughing out of frustration and what I probably looked like. Then I heard a pleasant whisper, "Mary." I looked up from my effort, thinking it was my beloved Joseph. He wasn't there. *I must be hearing things, and just wishing he were here. He will be so pleased with my first loaf of bread—I hope!*

Again, in a soft voice, "Mary." I looked up again. This time, I saw tiny specks of light that grew in brightness. It was beautiful and fascinating! Slowly, the particles multiplied and turned into a very tall and glorious being, but still almost transparent. I was spellbound, speechless, and a little frightened! Backing up, I tripped over one of my favorite baskets, but caught myself before falling flat to the floor.

"Greetings to you, Mary. You have found favor from the Lord, and are highly blessed—blessed above all other women," the awesome being said to me. *What is happening? Who is this stunning creature? What is happening? Is this... is this an angel?* How could I respond to such a statement as this? Words were stuck in my throat.

"Mary, don't be afraid," the angel said, kindly and smiling. "Because you have found favor with God, you will become pregnant and have a Son. You will call his name Jesus. He will be great and called the Son of the Highest. He will be given the throne of David and will rule over the house of Jacob forever. His kingdom shall never end."

Very timidly and in a whisper, I questioned, "How can this be? I am a virgin and have never been intimate with a man?"

"The power of the Highest shall cover you, making the holy child in your body to be called the Son of God." The angel had an engaging smile and looked so happy! His happiness made me smile too! (Even though I was smiling, I can't say I was *happy*.) What was happening here—happening now? After a few moments, he added, "Also, your barren cousin, Elizabeth, in her old age, is pregnant as well, and in her sixth month. Go to her."

What could I say? It was all so overwhelming and humbling. I don't remember getting on my knees, yet it seemed only right and appropriate for me to be kneeling. With my head bowed and bread flour still on my hands, face, and clothes, I timidly replied, "Whatever the Lord wants of me, I will do. I am only His poor, humble servant." As I was looking up, the lights slowly faded and the angel was gone! I felt tremendously blessed in having seen and talked to one of God's holy angels.

It took a while for my head and my heart to comprehend what had just happened. (Actually it took many years to *fully* understand.) The more I thought about it, the more excited and happy I became. *I must go to Joseph, and tell him the good news.* When I got to Joseph's workshop, he wasn't there; the door and windows were shut and locked. Running to the house, I asked Sara, "Where is Joseph? I went to his shop and everything is closed up."

I must have looked frightened because Sara had me sit down, saying, "My sweet child, rest yourself a moment and drink this cool water. Joseph will be gone for a couple of days; he is making a delivery of some chairs he made for a family west of here. Tell me, Mary, is there a problem?"

"No, I just needed to talk to him about something important, something rather *private.* I guess it will have to wait. I am leaving soon to visit my cousin, Elizabeth, who is pregnant. I don't know how long I will be gone. Will you tell Joseph for me?"

"Of course, my dear. Are you sure there is nothing else you want to tell him—or me?"

"Um…Um…No, but thank you." I wanted so much to tell Joseph the exciting news, but it would have to wait! I walked home slowly, now thinking of how I was to prepare for my visit to Elizabeth. She must be so excited and happy too!

When I told Papa I wanted to visit my cousin Elizabeth and that she was six months pregnant, he laughed. "Not Elizabeth, she is too old! What makes you think she is going to have a baby? Where did you hear such a thing?"

"Yes, Papa, I know she is very old. But an angel told me she is pregnant and now I must go to her. Please, may I go?" (I didn't tell Papa what *else* the angel said to me—not just yet, and not before I had a chance to tell Joseph the wonderful news.)

Papa stood for a while with his arms crossed and squinted at me as if he were trying to read my mind. I was afraid he would deny my request. Maybe he thought I was under too much stress in planning for my marriage to Joseph. Perhaps he thought I wanted to avoid my cooking lessons, or—I don't know. We both stood looking at each other, trying to guess what was on each other's mind.

Papa finally agreed to let me visit Elizabeth, "But your two brothers will travel with you on this journey—for safety, you know." I wasn't sure how long I would be gone, so I packed two of my favorite baskets, the ones with lids and handles. My brothers took turns carrying the heavier one and complained all the way! I don't think they really minded, but just wanted to tease me a little. That's what brothers do, I guess. I carried the food basket that Mama packed for us, since this journey would take two or more days of walking to the hill country of Judea where Elizabeth and Zacharias lived. Since I was a very young child the last time I saw my cousin, I didn't remember that it was *so far.*

I didn't tell my brothers my blessed secret. I wanted to, but thought Joseph should know first. *He will be so happy for us—I think. Anyway, I will give him the good news and tell him about the angel when I get back home.*

Walking into Elizabeth's house without my brothers, I said, "Greetings, Cousin! Do you remember me? I am your cousin, Mary."

In a clear and melodious voice, Elizabeth said, "Mary, you are blessed above all women, and blessed is the child you are carrying. Why am I so favored that the mother of my Lord is here to see me? Blessed are you, Mary, for believing what God has told you is going to happen."

The mother of my Lord? How does Elizabeth know? Who told her? Perhaps it was the same angel who came to me. I meekly, but joyfully replied, "God has chosen me, His humble servant, and all generations will call me blessed." Spending time with my cousin gave me such a blessing. It helped to strengthen my faith and helped me understand the great and wonderful responsibility placed upon me—and Joseph.

After about three months, (and more cooking lessons from Elizabeth) I felt the need to return home. Again, for safety, Elizabeth and Zacharias sent an escort with me back to Nazareth. Upon arriving home, Papa wanted me to tell him all that had happened during my visit. "Okay,

Papa, but *first* I must talk to Joseph. I have some very wonderful and glorious news for him." I ran out the door and over to the carpentry shop.

"Joseph! Joseph! I have wonderful news!"

He looked up and gave me a smile that weakened my knees. "Yes, I heard your cousin Elizabeth is having a baby, and in her old age. I am so happy for her, but I am especially happy that you are back home!"

"No—yes—no, but that is not the good news, Joseph. Joseph we are going to have a baby. A son!"

"I'm sure we will, Mary. Someday, we will have a child, but we cannot know for sure if it will be a *son*."

"Yes, we can, Joseph! Before I left to see Elizabeth, an angel told me I am pregnant and will have a Son. He will be the Son of the Highest, and sit on the throne of David. We are to name Him Jesus."

Joseph dropped the carpenter's tool he was holding and just looked at me. Frowning! *Why is Joseph frowning?*

"What? Mary, what…what's going on? What have you done?"

"I have done nothing! Well, yes, I talked to the angel and he told me—"

At that, Joseph turned his back and walked out of the shop. He didn't believe me! He didn't believe an angel told me I was pregnant and going to have a son! *What is he thinking? Does he think that I…? Oh, no! Can he possibly think that I…? How can I explain to him this is wonderful news?*

Tears welled up in my eyes. I loved Joseph so much, but I realized this "good news" was understandably incredible. It was to me too, at first! I guess I just assumed he would believe me and be happy we were chosen by God to raise His Son and the Savior of our people.

Was my life changed? Absolutely! Within the past few short months, I was promised to a man, a good man with four children. I was slowly learning to cook and enjoying it more than I expected. Then, the really big "change." An angel from God told me that I, a virgin, was going to have a Son who would one day sit on the Throne of David and rule forever. Praise God from whom all blessings flow! Yes, this is a tremendous change for me, and for everyone.

Joseph

Joseph
(The Obedient)

What was I to do now? Mary couldn't be *pregnant!* She didn't *look* pregnant. Of course, she said this all happened (talking to the angel and all), about three months ago before going to see Elizabeth. Could this really be true? Mary seemed so happy about it. Could she really be *that* naive? What will people say? I didn't believe her! In fact, I just turned and walked away from her. Others will probably do worse! Yes, what will they say? What will they *do* to her?

When I finally returned to my workshop, I was glad Mary was gone. I just couldn't face her right now. My head was hurting and spinning. My stomach was threatening to erupt. My whole body ached and I felt as weak as a willow. Weak as a lamb! Weak as a newborn—*baby!*

Up until now, I felt Mary was so pure, so sweet, so innocent, and I loved her deeply. Had she lost her sanity or had she betrayed me? What was I to do? Perhaps, she is wrong. Perhaps she is *not* pregnant. Time will tell in a month or two. Then I will have to make some decisions. In the meantime…

Mary and I didn't talk much now. She was hurt! I was hurt! Whenever I saw her in the garden, she didn't wave to me. She would nod and give me a slight smile. Sara asked, "Joseph, what is going on between you and Mary. I don't see you together and she seems distant. Have you done something to hurt her? She doesn't come by any more for cooking lessons? The children miss seeing her. I miss her. What is going on? Joseph! Talk to me!"

"Sara, it's between Mary and me. So for now, just drop it!" I didn't like talking to Sara like that, but I just could not speak of it now. Now or…I knew Sara would not drop it, and that her questioning and nagging would return in a day or two.

It seemed an eternity, but actually only a few weeks when it looked like Mary had put on some weight. Added weight on Mary's extremely thin body would normally be good for her, but not for the reasons she *gave*. Not for the reasons I *feared!* Now, I needed to talk to her. I sighed deeply. I felt like my *life* left my body.

After work and dinner (and at the nagging of Sara), I went to Mary's house. Mary's father answered the door and looked at me with narrow and glaring eyes. *Does he know Mary is pregnant, and is he blaming me?* Not looking directly at him, I muttered, "May I please speak to Mary?" Mary had been standing behind her father, and at my request, she came around slowly and timidly. He took a hold of her arm to prevent her from coming to me. She looked pleadingly at him. After a slight nod from her father, Mary stepped toward me.

Without talking, Mary and I went to the garden beside her house in the cool of the evening. We sat down on a rickety bench among the herbs. The silence between us was agonizing. Without our usual friendly small talk, I finally blurted, "I need to know about your—your pregnancy!" Mary looked innocently into my accusing eyes. Her eyes pooled with soft tears.

Then as if she could hear music or see angels, she opened up. Spilling with rejoicing. Mary now seemed to *glow*! With her eyes dancing, she told me again about the angel, about the promised Messiah, about the blessing placed upon *both* of us. Her words of exaltation overflowed. She seemed so happy and thrilled about it all. I found myself almost being caught up in her joie de vivre. *Almost!*

This was *not* realistic! This was not *possible!* With sad eyes and a crushed spirit, I said nothing! I stood up, took her small hand, walked her back to her front door. I left!

Now, I had to make some dreaded decisions. Decisions I knew that would be hurtful, especially to Mary. I still loved Mary so very much, but her being obviously pregnant and our marriage still a few months off, it became necessary for me to put together a resolution. *For Mary's sake, I will quietly and privately annul our betrothal. My heart is breaking!*

That night, before going to bed, I went into the house and lit the single oil lamp sitting on the table and called, "Sara, will you come out, please? I have something to tell you."

Sara emerged from the bedroom wrapping a shawl around her plump shoulders and trying to smooth down her unruly hair. Her first words were, "Well, it's about time, Joseph! Talk to me!" Sara sat down, but I couldn't. I paced! Not knowing how to start, and not looking directly at Sara, I just blurted, "Mary is pregnant."

"Yes, Joseph. I know! It is quite obvious she is pregnant. I am just very surprised and disappointed in Mary—and *you!* How *could* you?"

"Me?" I said in astonishment. "Her baby is not *mine!*" I didn't intend to be so accusingly blunt or mean-spirited! But, to be blamed for *this*? No!

Sara put her hand over her mouth as if holding back some ghastly words. Even in the dim light, I could see her inky-black eyes glaring at me. I knew she wanted to ask, "Who's baby is she carrying?" But she didn't. In a hushed voice (not her usual volume), she questioned, "What are you going to do, Joseph?"

"I don't really know. I am so confused. I love Mary deeply and sincerely, but this problem is beyond my understanding!" After a few moments, I added, "I will not humiliate her publicly, but I must have the marriage contract set aside quietly. That is what I will do, as soon as possible. Probably tomorrow morning."

I went back to my workshop and to my small cot in the corner. Normally, I would shake the wood dust and shavings from my clothes, but tonight I didn't care. I didn't care about anything. I didn't hang my clothes on the corner peg. Just let them fall to the floor, along with my tears. No pride. No dignity.

Again, I felt the wretched pain of losing someone I loved first my beloved Anna, and now my betrothed and sweet Mary. Out of my life. Both of them! My heart was breaking and I could not sleep.

"God, Oh God, please comfort me! Tell me what to do!" I was tired—bone-tired and sleepy, but sleep would not come to ease my pain. I tossed and turned, trying to get comfortable, trying to get some sleep. Thinking of the dreadful thing I had to do in the morning.

Just before dawn, it happened! The most amazing thing! My workshop filled with light, a bright but comforting light. It was too early for the sun. Suddenly, there stood before me a glorious and what I assumed a heavenly angel. He addressed me as, "Joseph, son of David." Now I was wide-awake!

Continuing, the angel said, "Do not be afraid to take Mary as your wife. She is carrying a Holy Child, a Son given to her by God. You will give Him the name of 'Jesus,' which means 'Savior', because He will save His people from their sins."

The angel stood for several moments, looking and smiling at me. I didn't speak and felt at a loss for words. I thought, *Am I supposed to say something now?* He didn't ask me anything. He didn't ask if I had any questions or concerns. He just told me what to do. A directive! He was very plain-spoken in his flat, yet sensitive and compassionate way.

Slowly, the light faded. He was gone! I still had questions—serious questions. But I knew what I must do now. I will go to Mary and beg her forgiveness. I pray she will forgive me for doubting and accusing her. Then without delay, if she will still have me, I will take her to be my wife.

After the sun was up and shinning in the windows of my workshop, I picked my clothes up from the floor and shook off the wood dust and shavings. I hadn't had any sleep, but I felt energized. I started to get dressed, but thought, *No, this will not do. I need to look my best for my apology. Hmm, what shall I wear? I don't have a large selection, but it should at least be clean!*

When I got to the house to select some clean clothes, Sara had a breakfast set for the children and me. "Thank you, but no thank you, Sara. I'll just have a piece of your wonderful bread. I am in a hurry to see Mary. I'll talk to you later." Out the door!

I was almost to Mary's house when I stopped short. *A gift. Yes, a gift! What can I give her?* I patted myself down as if I were looking for something *on* me. Ridiculous! *Flowers!* Yes, I should give her flowers. But I had often given her flowers. I wanted something *special.* Maybe, a *big* bouquet of flowers, the biggest I could collect!

I went to the hillside and found some very lovely wildflowers to pick—and pick. I picked so many, I could barely reach around their stems. Now off to Mary's house and hopefully back to her heart! I think I now understand her elation and excitement.

When Mary answered the door, I pulled the flowers from behind my back, held them out for her. I just grinned—and grinned. She looked mystified. Was it the flowers or my ear-to-ear smile that confused her? All I could say was, "Mary, will you walk with me? Will you talk with me?"

With a slight nod, Mary accepted my flowers, which needed both of her hands to reach around them. We walked to her herb garden and sat on that same rickety bench. I told her about my confusion, my doubts, and my pain. I told her about the angel coming to me during my restless and sleepless night. "It was probably the same angel that came to you, Mary."

We shared many thoughts, feelings, and fears for an hour or more. Then, the big question came from my trembling lips and heart. I stood up and said, "Will you please forgive me for my doubts about you, and the hurts I have inflicted upon you? Mary, *please* forgive me." Then taking her hand, I said, "Mary, I love you so very much, and I want you to be my wife and the mother to my children. Will you still agree to marry me?"

Mary stood timidly for several moments, then without saying anything, she reached up and flung her arms around me. She gave me a tender kiss on my cheek—my *first* kiss from my betrothed! What a surprise, what a delight!

"One more question," I added cautiously. "I know our marriage is a few months away, but will you marry me now? I mean tomorrow?"

"Yes, Joseph. I will marry you, but *tomorrow?* Of course, I will have to talk to Papa first, but under the circumstances, I think he will approve," she said smiling. "I have much to do before tomorrow, so I better be on my way—and talk to Papa!"

Now *I* needed to talk to Sara. She has been such a blessing to the children and me. Sometimes a pebble in my sandal, but nonetheless, still a blessing! I am sure she will understand and be pleased to move back into her own house.

After a couple of days' preparation with house cleaning, rearranging, and going to the priest for our marriage blessing, Mary moved into my humble house with my children and me! I am so happy!

Was my life changed? Again, yes! "Change" and stressors seem to be the norm for my life. Mary agreed to be my wife—a happy change. She became pregnant by the mystery of God—a confusing change. An angel told me to marry her anyway—a blessed change. Gossip and whispers by our friends and neighbors in Nazareth—a hurtful change.

Mary and Joseph

Mary and Joseph

Mary

Joseph and I had a simple wedding ceremony, trying to be as inconspicuous as possible because of my being obviously pregnant. Many eyebrows were raised. Hand-covered whispers. What did I expect? I should have anticipated such behavior, but it still caught me off guard and feeling defenseless. Even my own parents looked at Joseph and me differently. My husband became my rock and shield, but I could detect the hurt in his eyes too.

Joseph

I did my best to shelter and protect Mary from the disapproving eyes and whispers. We tried to stay away from the common activities of town, except for synagogue on the Sabbath. It was heartbreaking to see my children being the recipients of censure and teasing. We tried to manage as best we could (especially for the children's sake) to shelter our little family from all the malicious, small-town gossip.

Mary

Joseph's carpentry orders dropped off for a while, especially from the people in our village. But since he was known and recognized as a skilled craftsman, the orders from neighboring towns continued and even increased slightly. He enjoys his work and is gratified by making something both practical and appealing. I am so proud of him!

I was starting to waddle. The waddle of a very pregnant woman close to term! With Sara's help (bless her heart), I was able to keep up with my responsibilities of taking care of our four active children. She was keeping a close eye on me too, and making plans to be with me during the birth of our baby. She kept reassuring me, "Don't worry, Mary, I have done this hundreds of times!" I felt confident and comfortable being under the watchful care of Sara, until…

Joseph

A decree arrived from Augustus Caesar, the Emperor of Rome! Everyone throughout the vast Roman Empire had to return to and be registered in their own towns. Since I am a descendent of the house of David, I was required to go to Bethlehem to register. This would take several days travel from Nazareth. This decree seemed to send everyone in turmoil and suspicion. "What was this really about?" "Will our taxes increase?" "Will we have an added demand to support more Roman wars, more soldiers, and more iron rule?" Many were now making plans for travel to far off areas. Towns they probably had not been to for a long time, or possibly never.

Mary and I talked about what we needed do. She wanted to go with me, but I was reluctant and afraid the trip would be too much for her since this was close to her delivery time. And what about the children? We brought Sara into the discussion. Her first concern was, of course, for Mary. After thinking awhile, she clapped her hands together and said in her assume-control manner, "The Lord will take care of Mary. Do not fear! I will move back into your house and take care of your children. You know I love them like they were my own. We will be just fine!" The decision was made (mostly by Sara) and the discussion closed, as far as Sara was concerned. So that was that! We would leave the children with Sara while Mary and I made the long trip to Bethlehem. Papa loaned us his donkey.

Mary

The trip was long and tiresome, with lots of travelers on the road. I walked some of the way, but mostly I got to ride on Papa's donkey. We could travel a little faster if I rode. A couple of nights we were able to find simple lodging, but upon our arrival in Bethlehem, we found the city to be very noisy, busy, and crowded!

I didn't want to complain, but I said, "Joseph, I am so glad to *finally* be here. My back really hurts! Do you think you can find us a comfortable place to stay—and a cool drink of water?"

Joseph looked at me with narrow eyes, but said, "Yes, my beloved. You sit on this bench while I will get you a cool drink then I'll find us a room. Are you okay?" I didn't want to worry or lie to him. I just gave him a rather weak smile.

Joseph had to wait in line at the well for the water. When he returned, he looked stressed and said, "The rabbi at the well said we will have trouble finding lodging tonight. He said our best bet would be the inn a few doors down. He also offered to stay with you while I look for a room."

"Thank you, Joseph. Please hurry, I am not feeling very well." The rabbi came to my bench and kindly introduced himself, but I must admit I wasn't really listening. I was trying to get comfortable on the uneven and teetering bench. Certainly not the kind of bench Joseph would have made!

Joseph

I was really worried about Mary. She had the look of impending childbirth. I ran to the suggested inn, but there was a line there too. The innkeeper announced to the group that the inn was full. He shrugged and said with a half-smile, "Sorry!"

Everyone left the line except me! I walked up to the innkeeper and took a hold of his collar, I got very close to his face and looked deep in his eyes. He tried to pull away, but I had a strong grip. "Look," I said. "My wife and I have come from Nazareth, and have been traveling several days. She is about to deliver a baby! You have to have *something!*"

"Nope!" Again with, "Sorry!"

The innkeeper's wife was standing off to the side. I didn't notice her until she came forward saying, "About ready to deliver at baby, you say? Sir, I am so sorry about not having anyplace comfortable for you and your wife, but there is a stable up the hill behind our inn. I'll get a lamp and show you the way. Just follow me."

A *stable?* Running back to Mary, I found the rabbi still with her and looking concerned. "Sir, her time is near. I hope you found a room!" I shook my head slightly to the rabbi.

We helped Mary to her swollen feet, and I explained I found a *place* for us. "Not a room, exactly, but a place to spend the night. We have to follow the kind innkeeper's wife up the hill." I didn't want to tell Mary or the rabbi that it was a *stable*. We would have to share the lodging with papa's donkey and other animals!

The rabbi and I helped (and almost carried) Mary. Walking slowly, we followed the innkeeper's wife with the lamp up the narrow path. When we got there, she used her apron to shoo out some of the animals—chickens, pigs, and goats. There was no bed, but she pulled down a little fresh straw from a shelf, fluffed it up, and said with her hands on her hips, "There!"

I put some blankets down on the straw and helped Mary to lie down. All she said was, "Joseph! Joseph! Ooooh, Joseph!" I felt helpless. I wanted so much more than a shelter for animals with a bed of straw on the ground for Mary and our promised Son!

Mary

Thank God for Joseph and the rabbi! I could not have walked up the path by myself. I thought I was just *tired*, but then I realized our Son was on His way! "Joseph! Joseph, I need Sara!" With help from my attentive husband, I was eased down on to the blankets covering the straw. The rabbi put his arm around Joseph's shoulders and spoke quietly, saying, "Everything will be all right now. God is here, even in this stable, and He will take care of her." He then came to me, lifted my hand and gave it a tender kiss. Somehow, I felt reassured that we were in God's safekeeping. The rabbi blessed us and left.

The innkeeper's wife was named Tamra. She talked very fast and had an accent that made her hard to understand, but her actions showed me that she really cared. Her husband was a bit aloof and business-like, but he did as he was told to do! And she knew how to *tell* him! She and her husband made several trips back and forth, bringing us more blankets, food, and cool water. Tamra stayed with us but told her husband to leave! It was gratifying to know we were not alone. Yet I would have *preferred* to be alone with Joseph. Except, I also wanted Sara!

Everything was happening so fast—yet not fast enough. I really didn't know what to expect. When the women in Nazareth were having babies, I was always outside the room. Outside the attention! Outside the activity! Too young! Now I was having the baby and still too young; and I was the *center* of attention. The attention of Joseph and a stranger! "Sara," I cried in the dusty air. "Where are you when I need you *most*?"

A few hours later—a few *long* hours later—our beautiful Son was born! "Is that music I hear, Joseph? Where is it coming from? It's very faint and far away! Do you hear it too?" My dear husband looked too exhausted to hear anything. He sat near me with his head down, shoulders slumped, eyes closed, and tears spilling over. You would think *he* had just delivered a baby. Well, actually he had! I felt drained too, but euphoric and walking on clouds with swollen feet.

Tamra took charge of our newborn; cleaning, wrapping, and putting him in a little bed so we could get some much needed rest and sleep. Since there was no bed for our Son, she cleaned and put fresh straw in a manger, a feeding trough for the animals. "Perfect!" she said with her hands on her hips.

I was almost asleep when I heard Tamra, "Shoo!" some men at the entrance to our room. In the dim oil lamp, I could see they were a motley group of shepherds and probably wanted to use this stable. Joseph jumped up and explained to the men that we were using it for the night. He asked them politely if they would kindly go elsewhere.

Looking a bit puzzled, the older man with missing teeth, asked, "Pardon, sir. Has a baby been born here tonight?"

"Um...um...yes." Joseph said, cautiously eyeing the ragtag shepherds who were trying to look around and over his shoulders. "Yes, our baby cried a bit, but I didn't think it was loud enough to draw a *crowd!* I am sorry if we disturbed you. Please be quiet, my wife and baby are trying to sleep. What do you want?"

The older man, who seemed to be in charge, grinned his toothless smile at the others and said, "This is the place!"

Stepping forward, a younger and much taller man said, "Sir, we don't want to put you out none, but while we was tending our sheep, a huge crowd of angels suddenly showed up in the sky. And it made the whole sky bright as day. I tell you, sir, we was mighty afraid! Then one of the angels said we wasn't to be afraid, and he even told us to be *happy*! He said the Messiah, our promised Deliverer, was just born in Bethlehem and sleepin' in a manger. You shoulda heard the music they was singing! So that's why we been checkin' out the stables and found you folks here. If it's no bother to you, can we just take a little peek at you baby?"

Joseph looked quizzically at me, as if asking what we should do about the request. I smiled and nodded. Showing our newborn baby to a group of scruffy shepherds was a bit unnerving, but if heavenly angels announced His birth to them, then we should, by all means, grant their request. Tamra, our self-appointed protector, didn't look very happy about it and kept a very close eye on our "guests." She would not allow them to touch Him.

The shepherds gathered around with their hands folded up to their chests and looked into the simple manger. The youngest shepherd, who looked to be about nine or ten, slowly reached toward our baby, but was quickly reprimanded by the older ones. They appeared in awe, like they were in the presence of royalty—even a king on his throne. They hardly breathed, until one asked what we named Him.

"Jesus," Joseph said. "His name is Jesus."

"Jesus," one of them said and added, "I won't forget *that* name!" They bowed reverently to us, thanked us, and left, saying, "Praise to the Lord our God."

Tamra left too, but promised to find us a better place in town for the next few days, or for as long as we needed to stay in Bethlehem. Now we were hoping to get a little sleep before sunrise.

Joseph

"What a night!" It all seemed a dream until the sun shone through a small window; that exaggerated the dust particles. And, of course, the smell of stable animals! I still felt the sting and guilt of having Mary deliver our baby (a Holy Child) in such a lowly and unworthy place.

Having the rumpled shepherds tell of angels appearing to them and announcing the birth of our Son helped me realize we had not been forgotten or abandoned by God. Even in this simple shelter, we were given God's messengers and blessings.

Later that morning, and true to Tamra's promise, she returned to tell us she had found a house for us to use. It was small and to be shared by another young family, but much better than a *stable*!

After forty days and according to Jewish law, we went to Jerusalem for the dedication of our Son (His circumcision had already been done on the eighth day). The priest who performed the sacred ritual seemed aloof and indifferent. Just another pitiful and poor family! When we gave him our sacrifice of two turtledoves instead of a lamb, as allowed for poorer Jews, he just rolled his eyes.

The dedication and registration were over, and Jesus was sleeping in Mary's arms. We turned to leave when a very old man and woman stopped us. They said their names were Simeon and Anna, and they had been promised by God that they would see the Messiah before they died.

Mary

Simeon was very old, bent over, and walked with a staff. I wasn't sure he could even see where he was going, let alone "see the Messiah." Yet he tenderly took our baby from my arms and held Him up toward heaven. He said our Son would be a Light to the world, and would be the cause of the rise and fall of many. Then looking directly at me, he said that a sword would pierce *my* heart also. *What does he mean? Will I be pierced? Will my baby be pierced?*

Anna was very old and frail-looking, but had clear blue eyes under her wispy white hair. After briefly touching the head of our baby and looking closely at His tiny hands, she said, "These precious little hands will one day heal and one day be hurt." Then she put her wrinkled, twisted, and cool hands on my flushed cheeks and looked intently into my eyes. With tears filling around her eyes, she said, "God's blessings on you, little mother, take courage!"

Joseph

While we were in Jerusalem for the dedication, there was great excitement about a large entourage of men from the East. They were at Herod's palace. This was interesting, but Mary and I needed to return to our little and temporary home in Bethlehem. We also needed to start making plans for our return to Nazareth.

The next evening, this group of Easterners arrived in Bethlehem, and came to our humble home! Through an interpreter, they explained that they had seen His "star" and had come to worship the new King. With their heads bowed to the ground, they gave us many gifts. I had never seen riches like these and wasn't sure how to respond. There was nothing we could offer them but our surprised thankfulness. The next morning, they were gone.

As Mary and I were sleeping the next night, an angel appeared to me again. The same angel who told me to not be afraid to take Mary as my wife. He said, "Quickly, leave Bethlehem with Mary and the baby, and go to Egypt."

I wanted to say, "Egypt? Why Egypt?"

But the angel added, "King Herod will try to kill your Son. I will let you know when it is safe to return to Nazareth. Now, leave quickly!"

I woke Mary and explained what the angel said, and that we needed to leave "quickly" for Egypt. *Bless her heart! My pure and innocent wife never questions the word of God.* Packing up papa's donkey with our meager belongings and the gifts from the Magi, we left Bethlehem for Egypt. Egypt!

Have our lives changed? So much has happened, both exciting and wonderful. The most glorious change has been the birth of our Son—the new King of the Jews. When doubts or questions arise, God sends us gifts of events or people to strengthen our trust. Our Lord is perfect in His blessings and His timing. We may not understand fully, but we can know that "God is with us."

Gabriel
MF

Gabriel (The Messenger)

Lucifer's rebellion in heaven was subtle, slow, and virtually imperceptible. He was the highest, the brightest, the Son of the Morning, and the most honored of God's creation. Being the covering archangel, he was in the continual presence of God. He had a magnificent multi-toned voice, and led the massive angelic choir in praises to God. All of creation loved him. Because of his beauty, honor, and the admiration of the other created angels, pride gradually filled his heart. In his vanity, he desired to have a more exalted position and to put his throne higher than God's.

Concealing his true intent and feelings, he gradually convinced thousands and thousands of angels that he could give them more freedom, saying, "God's laws are too restrictive." With his tremendous influence, he expressed an elevated love for the angels, and gradually planted doubts in their minds about God's love.

God pleaded with Lucifer to change his conduct and return his loyalty, but his pride forbade him. Eventually, war broke out in heaven, which caused injuries on both sides! This conflict terminated with Lucifer, and the angels who sided with him, expelled from heaven. A very heartbreaking, but necessary decision made by the councils of heaven.

After Lucifer was banished, God gave me the honored position of covering archangel. Instead of singing *in* the choir, I now *led* the massive choir. My voice is not as majestic as the three combined melodious tones that we enjoyed hearing from Lucifer. His brilliance, both in appearance and intellect, are greatly missed, but peace and harmony returned in heaven.

In heaven, yes! But now, the earth was doomed to have conflict and confusion because the man and the woman, created in God's image, chose to believe the lies told by Lucifer—whose name was changed to Satan. Destruction and death was the destination of Adam and his descendants, unless a Savior's sacrifice could be made. A "Plan" was prepared and explained to Adam and Eve. And like Lucifer, they too were banished from their beautiful home—the Garden of Eden.

In the most Holy of Holies, the heavenly sanctuary, there is a massive throne. Three-thrones-in-one. Magnificent thrones for the three Persons of the Godhead—God the Father, God the Son, and God the Spirit. Holy angels are continually coming and going with assignments and messages! It is always a great honor to be given an assignment, any assignment. Many times, I was given special missions to give messages to God's people on earth, especially concerning events of the coming Messiah. This was always precious to me.

On one particular occasion, being summoned by the Father, I entered the throne room. Bowing low with my wings covering my face, I noticed one throne was empty. The Son was not on His throne, nor was He anywhere in the room.

"Gabriel, it is time! I have *the* most important assignment for you. It's time for the Plan to begin! I am sending you to earth with a significantly important and valuable message. You are to go to the small village of Nazareth in Galilee. There you will find a young virgin who is to be blessed above all women. She will bear and raise the most precious of heavenly gifts given to the human race."

Yes, I knew the Plan. I knew that God the Son was to be born on the earth as a baby and live without sin to save humanity. Oh, the wonder of it! Now I was chosen and *honored* to be sent to the earth to find the favored virgin, and announce the coming of the long-awaited Messiah! *But how will I know who she is? No doubt, the Father will tell me!*

As I neared Nazareth, I saw the color of soft music and an aura of sweet fragrance coming from a simple dwelling. There I found a young girl humming while attempting to make bread. She had flour all over the table, the floor, and herself. She looked like purity and innocence with flour in her hair and on her nose. *Can she be the "chosen"? She is so young!* I looked up and saw the face of God smiling. Smiling at me. Smiling at her. He whispered, "Her name is Mary."

I wanted to shout the good news, but realized my sudden appearance would terrify this young blessed one. I chose, instead, to softly call her name and appear to her gradually. "Mary," I whispered. She looked up smiling as if she were expecting me. But, not seeing anyone, she went back to her humming and bread making. Being very careful not to frighten her, I gradually presented myself as the soft illumination of diamond-dust. I repeated her name gently, "Mary."

As hard as I tried not to frighten her, upon seeing me now in full view, she drew a quick breath, stepped back, and nearly stumbled over a basket on the floor. "Don't be afraid, Mary. Because you have found favor with God, I come to you with wonderful news." (I could easily see why the Father chose this precious and innocent young woman to be the mother of her Savior—the Messiah.)

When I gave her the blessed news of her being the mother of a Holy Child, Son of the Highest and given the throne of David, she didn't argue with me. Nor did she ask for proof as her cousin, Zacharias had done. She asked only, "How can this be? I am a virgin and have never known a man."

I explained, "The power of the Highest shall cover you, making the Holy Child in your body to be called the Son of God." I wanted to wrap my arms and my wings around her to give her comfort and strength to believe but was not instructed to do so. I knew God would do the rest! From that moment on, a company of angels were assigned to protect Mary and the Holy Child she was carrying because God knew Satan would do what he could to destroy them both.

When her betrothed husband, Joseph, didn't believe that Mary was still a virgin and going to bear a Holy Child from God, I was sent again to Nazareth. This time I talked to Joseph and assured him that this baby she was carrying inside her young body was of the Holy Spirit. I added that he should not be afraid to take Mary has his wife. *Joseph is a good man!*

A few months later, Caesar Augustus had ordered a census to be taken of everyone in the Roman Empire, which included Palestine. Being from the house and line of David, Joseph was required to register in Bethlehem. But the time was drawing near for the Holy Child to be born, so Joseph took Mary with him. This was a hard trip for Mary, but she didn't complain and wanted to be with Joseph.

Mary sometimes walked beside Joseph and sometimes rode a borrowed donkey. They, of course, could travel faster if she rode. After a few days of travel, they arrived at Bethlehem. It was noisy, busy, and crowded, and they needed to find a place to stay. I could see the stress on Joseph's face. He was told of an inn that might have rooms still available. After giving Mary a cool drink of water, Joseph had her sit on a bench while he ran to the inn. I had one of the angels cloak himself as a rabbi and stay with her for comfort and protection.

When Joseph found the inn full with no rooms available, I looked up to heaven and saw God smiling. I didn't know the plan, but was assured that all would be fine. The innkeeper was cold and indifferent, but his wife softened to Joseph's pleading and explanation of his wife's imminent delivery. Bless her heart! She seemed to take charge of the situation. With the help of Joseph and the "rabbi," Mary was helped, almost carried, up a narrow path to a stable. *From throne room to stable? From surrounding holy angels to surrounding farm animals?*

All the heavenly angels were told that the plan of redemption needed God the Son to come to this earth. He would be born as an infant and live as a man. This was incredible to us and hard to understand. Yet the appointed time was near! Oh, so near!

The innkeeper's wife removed her apron to shoo the animals from the stable and tried to make a soft bed for Mary. *Here in a stable?* And again, I looked up to the Father who was smiling. *Is this part of the Plan? Shouldn't the Messiah be born in a more respectable and cleaner environment?* There was so much I wanted to do, and *could* do, to change the situation, but was not given permission by the Father.

Finally, He arrived! Tiny and helpless! His hands that once held the universe were now so tiny and could hold nothing. His mouth that created the earth by speaking was now crying. Omnipotence was now helpless. Helpless and vulnerable! This precious newborn Lamb of God was unaware of the love and excitement surrounding Him by the heavenly host. Unaware of the hate and fear that also surrounded Him by the dragon and his host. Unaware of the apathy which would turn to jealousy and hate by the "chosen" of God. Unaware of the struggle to save humanity from their sins. Unaware!

I wanted to touch Him, to hold Him! I even reached toward Him, but felt an unseen hand on my arm restraining me. *I know who this baby is, but does He know me? Can He even see me?* I finally realized I wasn't breathing, just holding my breath. I was in awe! I was a witness to the most amazing miracle, the Son of God, a human baby destined to save the human race. I looked around to the other angels. Some were gazing intently, some had their closed eyes in reverence, and some were crying.

I designated some of the angels to stand guard inside and outside the stable. The others, I motioned to follow me to the hillside above Bethlehem. My orders were to announce this blessed event to some simple shepherds.

Gradually, we began to show ourselves until the whole hillside was bright. Singing was just a natural response to our witnessing such a wonderful event. The shepherds were stunned and not just a *little* frightened! I told them, "Don't be afraid! I bring you and all people great news! Your Savior has just been born in the city of David. You will find Him wrapped warmly and sleeping in a manger." I wanted all four of these humble shepherds to look for the blessed baby, so I whispered to the oldest, "Go. I will tend your sleeping sheep."

In the midst of this exciting and blessed event, I was ever vigilant to the dangers of the powerful and malicious dragon. The whipping of his tail, the sinister threats, and the fiendish laughing could send terror down our spines if it weren't for the power of the Father being on our side. Since the beginning of Lucifer's rebellion, we understood there had been a controversy between Good and Evil, between God and Satan, between virtue and vice. Now was the zenith, the crowning moment, the decision, the Plan of Redemption for all humanity. And lying in a *manger!*

There were a lot of things to do—announcements and protections! When the Magi from the East arrived in Jerusalem, the "star" they had followed began to fade. They sent messages to Herod Antipas, asking for an audience and where they might find the newborn King of the Jews. Herod naturally expected his own son to be the next king, but also realized this decision would be made by the Emperor of Rome. After having the Jewish priests study the scriptures for any information regarding a new king foretold in prophecy, he told the Magi. "This baby and new king you are looking for will be found in Bethlehem, not far from here. After you find Him, report back to me that I may also pay him honor." This, of course, was a lie!

The entourage moved with haste to Bethlehem, the City of David. I, unseen, led them to a small and humble house where they found the King, the Savior of the human race! They presented their gifts to the surprised young family, and worshiped the newborn King. That night, I gave the Magi an urgent message. "Do not travel through Jerusalem on your return trip to the East, nor tell Herod where you found the baby. King Herod, in his jealous and drunken rage, will plan to search for and destroy the new King. Leave *now*—quickly." Before daylight, they broke camp, and planned a different route for their return trip. This, of course, infuriated Herod.

When Herod discovered he had been duped, he ordered the destruction of all baby boys in Bethlehem two years of age and younger. I was now given the order from the Father, "Go to Joseph and warn him. He must take his family and flee to Egypt." Joseph didn't question, but quickly obeyed and left during the cover of the night. *Joseph is a good man!*

Many, many times during the young life of Jesus, seen and unseen threats were made against Him. Satan could and would influence men to ridicule, humiliate, and injure the Son of God. There was so much I wanted to do for His protection, the protection I had the power to do, but I was limited by the Father who said, "He must endure, He must experience temptation, He must go through life as a human, and He must suffer for their sake."

The whole universe was watching this controversy. Satan continually accused God of being unfair and often pointed to the sins of those claiming to be His chosen people. Sins of lying, cheating, blasphemy, pride, idolatry, adultery, and murder were thrown in the face of God, saying, "I was kicked out of heaven for my rebellion, therefore fallen and rebellious man cannot be forgiven either. All sins have to be dealt with *equally*. Either overlook all sin or destroy all sinners. There is no such thing as justice *and* mercy! Either there is justice, which means death for all, or mercy, which is forgiveness for all sin."

The whole plan of salvation was explained to me by the Father, but it still remained a phenomenal mystery. I worshiped the Son of God in heaven, and now I worshiped the Son of Man on earth—a human! He was given my *limited* protection. The Father said, "His protection cannot exceed what is available to everyone for the asking."

Just before Jesus left His father's carpenter shop, He went to Mary, His mother. He put His strong arms around her, kissed her, and gave her a nod—a nod of thanks, a nod of love, and a nod of "It's time." He turned and walked down the dirt path with puffs of dust drifting with each step. With tears in her eyes, Mary knew that Jesus must leave the carpenter's workshop of His earthly father, and begin the work of His Heavenly Father. She was so proud of her Son. Still, she hated to see Him go!

Occasionally, during the ministry of Jesus, I was given special permission to intervene. But mostly, He relied on His closeness to the Father. My honored responsibility to watch over the Son of Man while on this earth was both sorrowful and joyful, a tremendous honor. It broke my heart to see His suffering and rejection. And yet, it was thrilling to see His faithfulness to the Father and His love for humanity.

At the beginning of His ministry, Jesus was led by the Sprit to the wilderness to be tested by the devil. He was there for forty days (without food) in earnest communication with the Father. Toward the end of those days, Satan came to Him as a beautiful and shining angel of light to "help and comfort" Him. He tempted Jesus with three suggestions, and always used that tiny word of doubt—"If." "If You are who You claim to be, then..." Not by any thought or action did Jesus yield to the temptations or suggestions by Satan.

His final days on this earth were the culmination of everything that is good in heaven and evil on the earth. Jesus was aware of His final destiny and tried to prepare His closest friends. Still they thought He would establish His kingdom on this earth, and they bickered among themselves about who would be chosen to sit closest to Him on His throne. At the Passover supper, all of them pledged their devotion except one. That *one* sold himself to the complete control of Abaddon—Satan, the devil.

When Jesus' disciples were too weak to offer Him comfort in the Garden of Gethsemane, I agonized with Him. His suffering was tremendously intense. So intense was His anguish, He might have died there, on the ground and alone, but that was not in the Plan. I looked up to God and pleaded with my eyes and my heart to help in some way. A smile and a nod were given to me from the Father. Kneeling beside the Prince of Peace, I lifted His precious head and wiped away some of the sweat and blood from His face. The cup from which He was about to drink trembled in His hands. Steadying His hands in mine, I was allowed to give Him encouragement and comfort for the final trial. It was a heartbreaking experience, yet, such an honor and a privilege! A privilege any one of His friends might have experienced if they had stayed awake and prayed.

As the closing scenes progressed, tension was increased. I realized what was in store for Jesus, and had asked the Father if there was anything I could do to relieve His suffering. His friends were no help! They were afraid for *themselves* and ran for their lives—rejecting and betraying Him. They scattered and hid from the Romans and the Pharisees. The Jewish leaders were afraid of losing their position and power, and the Roman rulers were afraid of a Jewish revolt. Fear was all around, but I was told by the Father, "Do not be afraid." Yet, *I can't help my feelings of tension.* I, and every angel in heaven, had offered to take the place of Jesus. But we were told our sacrifice would not be sufficient to save mankind.

Most of the tension and terror was expressed by Satan and his demons. The dragon seemed to get larger and more threatening.

Threatening all of God's creation! If Jesus died without submitting to even a small evil or selfish thought, Satan knew he would be lost forever. He would no longer be the king of this earth. He and his minions would be destroyed!

Satan wielded tremendous power and control over the farce trials of Jesus by the Sanhedrin, Herod, Pilate, the drunken and cruel soldiers, and the riotous mob. But who had the *real* power? With just a *look* or a flash of His divinity, Jesus could destroy everyone and save Himself. Even I had the *power* to end this cruelty. In Satan's immense and demonic power, he did all he could to convince Jesus that His sacrifice for humans was unacceptable and even displeasing to the Father.

While hanging on the cruel and ignominious Roman death device, Jesus cried to the Father. "Why have You forsaken Me?" All the sins of mankind were hanging on that cross, and the *sins* were the only thing that the Father despised. In fact, the Father, with tears running down His own face, was right next to the Son. As I looked around, with tears beclouding my eyes, I longed to take away Jesus' pain and His fear of separation from the Father. All the heavenly angels were crying too.

The only comfort Jesus received while hanging between heaven and hell, came from one of the other condemned men. He didn't ask Jesus to save him from the cruel death, but "Remember me when You return with Your kingdom." I saw a brief but heavenly smile spread across the tortured and bleeding face of the Son of Man, and a word of promise from His lips.

After several long hours, Jesus called out in a voice stronger than expected of a dying man. "It is finished." He then breathed His last and closed His eyes. It was indeed "Finished." Heaven was silent, empty, no music, no singing. Stunned silence!

As far as I could tell, Jesus did all that He and the Father proposed thousands of years earlier to save mankind when Adam and Eve failed their test. *At least now, Jesus' suffering is over!*

Suddenly, it seemed that all of creation rebelled at the death of its Creator. Darkness covered the earth, lightning flashed, hitting trees, buildings, and mountains. The earth shook violently, spitting out some of the dead from their graves. But louder than all of the thunder and earthquake, was the yelling of the furious dragon, the condemned devil. His evil demons scattered like rats and hid like cockroaches in the light.

Tenderly, a few heartbroken friends of Jesus took Him down from the cross, washed His body, and laid Him in an unused and unfinished tomb. Their hopes were crushed with His death. Their hopes of crushing Rome were gone. Their beliefs that Jesus was the Son of God were dashed and buried with Him. *No! Don't you remember His words? Don't you remember He told of His death, and that He would rise again on the third day?*

Early on the third day, before light, I was given the honor of telling Jesus, "The Father calls you." I just couldn't stop smiling! Such a joyous and thrilling event! Jesus sat up then stood. The burial clothes fell to the floor. I handed Him clothes to put on for His reentrance into the world. After dressing, He folded His burial clothes. So like Him! Perfect in every way! Then, I knelt down and worshiped the Son of Man—the Son of God. After giving me a Son-of-Man-like hug, He said, "I must now go to the Father."

I stayed behind in the empty tomb to tell those looking for Jesus' body that He had been risen from the dead! *Jesus Himself had raised several people from the dead, why are His friends having such difficulty believing He is alive?*

Ten thousand times ten thousands of angels accompanied Jesus to the pearly gate of heaven. God the Father was waiting for Jesus. The sacrifice of Jesus was accepted, and the human race could be given salvation and eternal life to all who love Him. All heaven worshiped and gave Jesus honor.

Has my life changed? No! However, my understanding and my appreciation have grown for the tremendous sacrifice made by God, not only for men on earth, but to prove His love to the whole universe. I may never fully understand, but will have eternity to study the plan of salvation for fallen man. If man could see a small portion of love that God has for them, and what God has in store for them in heaven, they would say, "Our sacrifice, our suffering is a small price to pay for eternal life with Jesus Christ our Lord and Savior."

Balthazar

Balthasar (The Magi)

My name is Balthasar from Arabia but currently residing in Persia with an old astrologer and friend, Melchior. I have always been fascinated and interested in studying the stars. Even as a young lad, I read all I could get a hold of from the Greek astronomer, Hipparchus. I studied his star catalogues that organize astronomical objects. Oh, how I wished there were some way of seeing the heavenly bodies closer and clearer. Maybe someday...but for now, I will gaze upward and observe. And I will document the differences in brightness or movements.

One night, I became aware of a particularly bright star. Why hadn't I noticed this before? Over the next few days, it seemed to be getting brighter. *Fascinating! What does this mean?* Melchior, being very old and very wise, studied the stars *and* history—especially Hebrew history. He said there were several references to a star that foretold of a new King, and the time setting seemed to coincide with this star. We studied and watched this phenomenon.

When the star began to move slowly westward, we decided to follow it. Extensive preparations were made as this trip would probably take many months, perhaps a year, to arrive in Judaea. Another young astrologer, Caspar from India, joined us. Our entourage was large with servants, provisions, and gifts.

Upon our arrival in Jerusalem, it was not surprising that the city seemed curious and troubled. Our large group of foreigners caused quite a stir. However, it *was* surprising that Jerusalem was not joyous and celebrating the birth of their long-ago-promised Messiah, and King of the Jews. Even the religious leaders seemed indifferent and suspicious to our inquiries. Had we made a terrible mistake, were we completely wrong in our studies and convictions?

After a couple of days, our request for an audience with King Herod was granted. Through our interpreter, and according to oriental custom, we presented many gifts to the king. With the social obligations and courtesies out of the way, we presented our request. "Where is He that is born King of the Jews? We have seen His star in the East and have come to honor Him."

It was difficult to read Herod. His face appeared disturbed and hard, but his voice and words, through our interpreter, sounded genuinely sincere in helping us find this new King. A cunning and wily fox! We were told we could find the Child in Bethlehem, which we already *knew*, but needed authorization to travel through Herod's jurisdiction. He then asked us to report back to him where we found this new King, so he could *also* worship and honor Him.

Upon arrival in that little town of Bethlehem, it seemed we were supernaturally "led" to a small and simple house. There was no royal guard to protect the new king at this ignoble dwelling. Certainly not what we expected for the new King of the Jews!

Again, through our interpreter, we presented our many riches and gifts to the Child, the new King of the Jews. These poor, peasant parents were astonished and speechless! Finally, with gracious manners, this humble family bade us farewell and safe return to our countries.

That night, the star was greatly faded and nearly gone, and we realized we had indeed accomplished our mission. Now, through dreams, all of us were warned not to return through Jerusalem and tell Herod of our find because he would plan to destroy anything or anyone who threatened his throne. We were told to return to our countries by a different route, which we did!

This experience remained with me for many years. Realizing the new king must now be well into His adulthood, I decided to search for Him again. Now as an old man myself, and taking only one servant with me, I again traveled the many miles back to Jerusalem. I arrived at the end of the Jewish Passover period. It was crowded and noisy and not what I expected for a Holy week. Then I heard shouts and chanting, "Make way for the King of the Jews!" *Wonderful! Marvelous! History is complete!*

I followed the crowd, and discovered the shouts and chants were not of jubilation, but for ridicule and mockery! *What is happening? Is this "King of the Jews" the one that I saw many years ago in Bethlehem? Surely, this Man is not the same person that was foretold in Hebrew scripture to rule Israel!* What I saw made me sick to my stomach. A Man condemned by Rome and on His death march to be crucified. Many people were jeering and mocking. Some were silent, subdued, and crying. I followed the crowd.

I was drawn to this Man and His suffering. His silence in the face of extreme cruelty. His forgiveness for his abusers. His compassion for His mother. His pity and hope for a fellow sufferer. The lightening, the earthquake, the screams of terror, and the testimony of a Roman centurion saying, "Surely, this Man was the Son of God."

After all of this, I stayed around for a few days questioning myself, questioning the past of thirty-some years ago. I looked for someone, *anyone*, who might be able to tell me about the Man who was crucified by Rome and hailed "The King of the Jews." There seemed to be so much secrecy and paranoia among those who knew Him. Finally, it was told to me that this Man, named Jesus, was alive—raised from the *dead!* I earnestly looked for Him, and eventually found Him among some of His followers. Bowing and introducing myself, I explained that I had come from the East, *twice*, looking for Him—the King of the Jews.

Jesus reached out and took both of my old and wrinkled hands in His scarred and nail-pierced hands. He then said with kindness and love, "Thank you. Go back home and tell others!"

Has my life changed? My life has been tremendously affected by both events of this Man. At His birth, His death, His resurrection! I, of course, am not Jewish, but I am determined to study deeper into the Hebrew Scriptures. Perhaps, even I may be given the hope and grace of a future Heavenly Kingdom, and see Him as King of kings.

John

John (The Baptist)

The earliest memories of my childhood come from the stories my parents told me about an angel visiting my father, Zachariah, while he was doing his duties in the temple at Jerusalem. My father was very old, as was my mother, who was barren. He was told by an angel that they were to have a baby. And this child would grow up to be a forerunner of the coming Messiah.

Even though my parents had often prayed for a child (and for the coming Messiah), my father didn't believe the glorious angel standing before him at the altar in the sanctuary. Because of his doubt, he was struck dumb and unable to talk until after my birth.

I was dedicated as a Nazarene from birth—consecrated to the service of God, to abstain from strong drink, and let my hair grow. It was naturally expected that I be educated for the priesthood and taught by the rabbis. Instead, I was taught at home by my parents, and prepared for my mission.

Since my parents were very old at my birth, I was a young man when they died. Not being sheltered by them any longer, I went to the wilderness to be taught by God and learn more from His nature. I wanted to avoid the love of luxury and greed for riches which were so prevalent in our society. I wanted to avoid temptation and stand for reformation. Elijah's simple clothing was what I chose for myself—a garment made of camel's hair and a leather belt.

"Temptation?" Do you think I wasn't tempted? I suffered cold, heat, hunger, wild animals, and loneliness. Keeping my mind on my God and my God-given mission was my only joy and peace.

Occasionally, I went into Jerusalem to study the prophetic scrolls about the coming Messiah and observe how best to reach men's hearts with God's message. It was sad to see the extreme social divisions. The display of wealth and status next to abject poverty and hunger. Many on all levels had physical diseases brought on by gluttony or malnutrition, by over indulgence or severe need. Returning back to the barren hills and rocky caves was a welcome escape from society's pointless activities, suspicion, and discontent.

When I was impressed to begin my mission, Judah and Israel were under complete Roman rule. "The Iron Rod of Rome!" The governors were suspicious of any unrest and intolerant of insurrection. Thousands of Israelis were executed.

My mission was to announce the coming Messiah and to *prepare the way*. I was not to preach a Roman revolution, but a revolutionary change of heart. Sometimes I was asked, "Are you Elijah?" Or, "Are you the Messiah?" Always, I would respond that my mission was only to prepare the way for the coming Messiah. The time was near!

My mother often told me of her first meeting with the mother of Our Lord. What a thrill that must have been for her! Even though I knew the Messiah and I were cousins, I had never met Him.

The Jordan River was an ideal place for speaking to large groups of people. Some were sincere and some were curious. I baptized many, which was the washing away of sins and the public dedication to God. Even some scribes and Pharisees were baptized, if only to impress the crowds of their integrity since my message was gaining much popularity. From fear of the people, I was often *privately* questioned or challenged by the Pharisees, but they would not openly support my message. They seemed to realize that eventually they would have to approve or denounce my work. Right now, they were taking the middle road. They were neither condemning nor condoning my message.

One day, while baptizing those who came to the Jordan banks, I saw Him. There was something special, something pure, something peaceful about this Man. He had an aura of Holiness, and was dressed in homespun attire. He smiled at me like we were old friends and walked up to me standing in the water. I took a step back. Catching my breath, I whispered to Him with my head lowered, "How can I baptize You? I am a sinner, and You are sinless! Baptism is for repentance of sin and guilt! Please, Lord, I need to by baptized by You."

Taking my hand in His, He placed His other hand on my shoulder. Looking deep into my eyes, He said, "This is necessary for fulfillment of all righteousness." Then guiding Jesus into the deeper Jordan waters, I "buried" Him, as I had done all others requesting baptism. An experience most exhilarating and humbling for me!

Upon coming up out of the water, a bright light shone all around Jesus. Then something that looked like a dove hovered above His head. And the voice of God said, "This is my beloved Son, in whom I am well pleased!"

Pointing to Jesus, I shouted to the crowd, "Behold the Lamb of God. He and only He will take away the sins of this world." All eyes of the hushed crowd followed Him as He walked away. He walked with resolve, with dignity, with purpose.

Later that day, two of my disciples, Andrew and John, who were good and sincere men, asked the meaning of *Lamb of God.* I encouraged them to look for Jesus and follow Him, adding, "He must increase, and I must decrease."

A month or more later, Jesus came by the Jordan again, from the wilderness area. This time, Andrew and John left me to follow Jesus. "Is this truly the Messiah?" they asked each other as they followed from a cautious distance. I wanted to follow Jesus too, but that was not my purpose. My mission and dedication were to point *to* Him and prepare believers for *His* service. Therefore, I continued to preach to the crowds and baptize many.

I was kept well informed of the popularity of Jesus while my influence waned. I now got open hostility from the Pharisees and the Sanhedrin. Most of my preaching was in the territory ruled by Herod Antipas, the son of Herod the Great, who was loosely related to Jews but was given his throne through Rome. When I denounced Herod Antipas's marriage to his brother's ex-wife, I expected my life might be in danger and my work ended. Sure enough, I was arrested and thrown in prison. *Being used to the open spaces of the hills and countryside, this dark and dank cell is very oppressive and discouraging to me.*

Occasionally, Herod would secretly come and talk with me. He seemed convinced and convicted of his sin, but too proud to confess or correct his life. I heard through the guards that his wife, Herodias, was threatening him. He stopped his visits.

As the weeks dragged on, I am ashamed to say that my faith faltered, my trust weakened. Since I was able to have visits from my disciples, I asked them to go to Jesus and ask Him if He truly was the Messiah, "Or should we look for another." Surely, *He* would save me from this terrible place. They came back with wonderful stories of miracles and healings. *My faith is restored! My hope is renewed! My strength has returned!*

While still in this dark prison, I am hoping for my release. Since Jesus has done wonderful miracles for many people, perhaps He will come for me. I must trust God and wait! In the meantime and for the last couple of days, I have heard in the distance lots of music, dancing, and laughing. And, no doubt, lots of drunkenness! It is Herod's birthday, and he is giving himself quite an elaborate party!

Has my life changed since knowing Jesus, the Messiah, the Son of God? Meeting Him, baptizing Him, and preparing for His ministry has been my life's service and greatest joy. I don't know what is in store for me in this dark and foul cell, but I can now say that I believe in Him and trust Him fully. I will one day see Him again, face to face—in this life or the next.

Peter

Peter (One of the Twelve)

If anyone were to ask you to name the disciples of Jesus, whose name would you think of first? Peter, right? Yes, that's me, Peter. Somehow, I seem to be named first, or at least among the firsts. Certainly, I was not the best nor did I have the most admirable attributes and characteristics of a disciple of our Lord. You probably would think of me as being the most self-assured and the most outspoken! Perhaps. I was a self-appointed spokesman, which often got me into trouble.

My brother, Andrew, and I were fishermen. We were not rich, but I owned our boat and we made a comfortable living. I always carried a long knife, mostly for cleaning fish! I was older, taller, and stronger than my bother. Our taxes were heavy, and we often talked about the coming Messiah who would put an end to our being *ruled* and oppressed by Rome. The coming Messiah was often the topic of conversations among all Jews. We hated Rome and the feeling was mutual toward us.

Andrew and I were often drawn with the crowd to the Jordan River where a man named John, called the Baptist, was preaching about the Messiah. He preached how we should change our lives; and he baptized many for the service of God. We began to believe that Jesus, who had been baptized by John, was the Messiah. The promised Savior of the Jews and our King to overcome the oppression of Rome.

I traveled from town to town with Jesus, learning from His stories and witnessing His healing of the sick or lame. The crowds were sometimes oppressive. The Jewish leaders and Pharisees were continually trying to maneuver Him into saying something they could hold against Him.

They seemed jealous of His popularity in influence. They were, of course, careful not to *openly* oppose Jesus for fear of the people.

Those of us who were closest to Jesus, believed that He would soon break out of His social position of poverty, and set up His powerful kingdom. I loved the Master and wanted to be with Him and sit beside Him when that happened! Occasionally, however, Jesus referred to His rejection, His betrayal, and even His death. This talk was irritating and galling to me, and I finally told Him so! "No! Don't talk like that! Don't even *think* like that! It will *never* happen!" I was willing and *ready* to fight or die for Him.

Shock! He called me Satan. *Me—Satan!* He said for me to get behind Him because I was an offense to Him! What? I believed in Him and His Kingdom and wanted to help Him. (It was sometime later, of course, when I realized His strong rebuke was not directed to *me*, but to Satan himself—the Devil.)

One time, after fishing all night and catching nothing, we pulled to shore. Jesus was standing there; the people were pressing all around Him. He stepped into my boat and asked me to pull away from the shore a little so He could easily be seen and heard by the *whole* multitude.

I was feeling discouraged and worn out because of fishing all night without success. Also, the thought of John the Baptist, imprisoned in a dungeon by Herod, weighed heavily on my mind. The priests and Pharisees didn't support Jesus and even showed malice toward Him. What did the future hold? All these thoughts were running through my mind as Jesus finished His preaching and dismissed the people. I sat slumped and tired in my boat when Jesus said to row out farther. I didn't know why but did as Jesus requested.

Upon reaching a distance from shore, Jesus said to drop down our fishing nets. *Really? It is midday and everyone knows fishing is best done at night. If we didn't catch any fish last night, how can we catch any now? But—why not?* We tossed the net over the side of the boat and caught a *miracle!* More fish than we had caught in many days! That "miracle" was not due to any belief or faith on my part. In fact, I *doubted* it! I now realize that Jesus was wanting to get my *attention!* Yes, He got my attention! We left the boat and the fish and followed Jesus. We became fishers of men!

Another time, a miracle happened during a horrible storm. After Jesus had fed five thousand people with a few loaves of bread and sent them home, He told us to get in a boat and go to the other side of the lake. He said He would meet us there later. While on our way, a sudden violent storm arose. Andrew and I, and some of the others, were strong seamen and had dealt with storms before. But we were being tossed about like a leaf in the wind. There was nothing we could do, but hang on. We feared we might drown.

Suddenly, we saw what looked like a ghost walking on the water, among the high waves. An omen of death! An augur to the watery grave! Then one of the men shouted, "It is the Master!"

I don't know why, (my mouth moves faster than my brain), but I called out and asked if I could go to Him. Jesus said, "Come." Yes! Yes, I was given permission by Jesus to walk on the water *with* Him. Before I stepped out of the boat, one of the men grabbed my garment to hold me back. I just pushed his hand away and kept going. I wanted to go to Jesus. What an exhilarating experience! Me—walking on water! *Me!* I looked around to see if the others were watching. Watching *me!* Then it happened! Splash! Down I went! I came up sputtering and called out to Jesus to "Save me!" Instantly, His hand caught hold of mine. Back to the boat we walked. Together! Jesus was dry, but I was soaking wet! I sat at the aft of the boat, cold and shivering, but glad to be alive. Quiet and humbled!

At Passover time, the Passover supper had been prepared for us in an upper chamber. The table was set. All was ready, except for the servant. It was customary for a servant to wash the dusty feet of dinner guests before the meal. *So, where is the servant?* All was silent and a bit uncomfortable as we looked around the group. Who would wash our feet? Who would humble himself to a servant's status? Certainly, not me!

Slowly, Jesus walked over to the basin of water. He picked up the pitcher, the basin, and a towel, and motioned for us to sit down. I am not sure, but I think He washed the feet of Judas first. It was all very silent. No talking! No whispering! A sacred and humbling experience. But when He came to me…my mouth—Oh, my mouth! Of course, I objected. "I am not worthy, my Master, of having You wash *my* feet." Ashamed! I was ashamed that I had not offered to wash *His* feet. When He told me I could have *no* part with Him unless He washed my feet, my mouth blurted for Him to wash not only my feet, but my whole body as well.

During the supper, Jesus said one of us would betray Him, and *all* would be offended and abandon Him. "Not me!" Somehow, I needed to convince Him of my sincerity. "Others might be offended, but I will *not!*" I said forcefully. I was sincere, but did not realize my weakness. I was strong physically but proved to be spineless. Feeble and frail in character! Still, I boasted of my resolve to stand with my Lord at any cost and in all circumstances.

It hurt me terribly when Jesus turned to me and said, "You, Peter will deny me three times, even *tonight!*" No! How could I do such a thing? He, of course, knew me better than I knew myself.

After supper, we went to The Garden—a place where we often went to pray. Jesus seemed especially burdened and occasionally stumbled. We needed to support Him while He walked. Upon arrival, He asked us to pray while He went a little farther to pray alone. I prayed. Yes, I prayed, but they were short prayers. It was late at night, and I was tired and sleepy. It had been a long day! I fell asleep leaning against a tree.

Shortly, Jesus came and asked why we were sleeping. He asked us *again* to pray. My prayers were again short and halfhearted. *Why can't I stay awake and pray as my Lord asks me?* Again, sleep overcame me!

Suddenly, there was loud shouting. *Now,* I was awake! A rowdy group of Roman soldiers, along with the temple police, were coming into the garden. Judas was leading the company. He ran to Jesus and kissed Him on the cheek. When the crowd got rough and someone bound Jesus' hands, I thought, *Here's my chance to prove my loyalty to Jesus.* I drew my knife and started swinging it. I cut off the ear of the high priest's servant. He screamed in pain. Confusion was everywhere! Hadn't I done well by standing up for Jesus, or was that wrong?

The strong cords binding Jesus' hands instantly fell to the ground. With tender compassion, Jesus put the ear back on the man. The only trace of the previously severed ear was the blood on the man's neck and clothes. He then stepped back away from the crowd. Maybe he left. I never learned what happen to him. Did he see the love in Jesus' eyes? Was he a changed man? If I could see him now, I would like to say, "I am sorry."

After Jesus' hands were bound again, *all* of us ran. Ran away! Ran in fear! Ran for our lives! Where was *my* loyalty? Where was *my* bravery?

Where was *my* willingness to fight and *die* for Jesus? Yes, I ran, but stayed as close as I dared—at a *safe* distance.

Jesus was taken to the Sanhedrin to be tried. Tried for heresy! Tried for blasphemy! Tried and condemned in the eyes of Caiaphas and the Jewish leaders. The "trial" was at night, which was illegal by Jewish law, and a farce! I stayed close enough to hear what was going on, but far enough away to appear unconcerned and indifferent to the proceedings. It was cold, just before dawn. I stood by a fire pit to keep warm, but I was still shivering. Shivering from the cold, from fear, and from shame. A woman asked, "Aren't you with that man being tried?" Everyone looked at me. I felt confused and pretended not to understand then replied angrily, "Woman, I don't know Him."

I was mystified as to why Jesus would submit himself to this humiliating treatment. Not just mystified, I was angry at His composure and His calm. *Why doesn't He do something to save Himself?* I tried to hide my true feelings by contributing to the jeering when the *second* accusation came that I was somehow connected to Jesus. This time I answered with a disgusting oath, and added, "I do *not* know the man!"

The third accusation really angered me! I flew into a rage with cursing and swearing. At the last denial of my Lord, a rooster crowed and Jesus turned to look at me. Our eyes locked. No condemnation, no hate. Only sadness—the sadness in His eyes was for me. *Me!* This man who knew me better than I knew myself. My boasting turned to shame. Strength turned to brokenness.

I could bear the scene no longer, and I left! I left half running, staggering, and stumbling. I found myself back in the Garden of Gethsemane, and shame brought me to my knees. My Lord could endure the words that were stabbed into his body by those who hated him, but more painful must have been my words of denial. My betrayal had twisted the knife! I didn't want to see anyone or talk to anyone. I just wanted and *needed* to be alone! Alone in my own pain and brokenness! I wanted so desperately to ask for His forgiveness. Forgiveness from Jesus and from God the Father! Since Jesus knew me so well, did He know how sorry I was? I wished I could take it all back! Would I *now* have to courage to stand beside Him at His trial? *I don't know!* I was not as sure of myself as I had been just a few hours earlier.

Jesus was tried and found guilty of blasphemy by Caiaphas and the Sanhedrin. Then He was tried by Herod and Pilate for treason. Jesus was not found *guilty* of treason, but was sentenced to be crucified to satisfy the demands of the mob. Crucified by Rome at the demand of the Jews! I am so ashamed of myself and my Jewish nation!

Early on Sunday morning, John and I were together, grieving and talking over the past couple of days, when Mary Magdalene came running to us and crying, "They have taken our Lord, and I don't know where He is. He is not in the tomb!" What? John and I ran to the tomb to see for ourselves. Being a much younger man than I, John got there first. Mary followed. Yes, the tomb was empty, except for the burial clothes, which were folded neatly at the foot. If Jesus were stolen, why would someone unwrap Him and *fold* the clothes?

I suggested that we go to the upper room where I thought the others might be; the last place where we felt close to our Lord. Where else could we go? Where else would it be safe to hide? Would there be safety in numbers? We all shared the same guilt of running away, but I knew my guilt was deeper. My eyes were still red and swollen as we cautiously walked through the streets of Jerusalem and met with other disciples. The upper room, which was used previously for the Passover supper, was now a hiding place. A secret meeting place! We were too afraid to be seen for fear of the Romans and the Pharisees. Now that Jesus was dead, would they be looking for us?

It seemed everyone was talking at once. We had already heard a report that Jesus' body was missing—"stolen by His disciples." All of us jumped when, suddenly, there was a knock at the door. After identifying who knocked, we cautiously unbarred the secured door. Two of our group came in and said they had talked to Jesus. Talked to our risen Lord! Was that true? Could the crucified and buried body of Jesus actually be alive? We knew His body was missing from the tomb, but *alive?*

Then suddenly, in the midst of our fears and crushed hopes, Jesus appeared! Gently reassuring us that He was indeed alive, He asked us for food to eat. Convinced, we touched, we hugged, we worshiped. I, however, fell at His feet, and I begged for forgiveness! With His nail-pierced hands, He lifted me from the floor and gave me a Savior-sized hug. *Never again will I deny my Lord.*

Weeks later, while eating food that Jesus prepared for several of us at the seashore, Jesus asked me if I loved Him. I answered Him, not in the boastful manner that I had once declared my loyalty to Him, but said, "Yes, Lord, You know that I love you." A few moments later, Jesus asked me *again* the same question. Again, I said I loved Him!

When Jesus asked me the *third* time if I loved Him, I was *crushed!* I felt awful! I had denied my Lord three times in His hour of need. So now I *needed* to declare my love and loyalty to Him—three times! *Yes, I can truly say, "With the help of God, I will never again deny my Lord and Savior!"*

Has my life changed? Since Jesus went back into Heaven, I have spent my life telling all who I meet of Jesus Christ and the Good News of His salvation. We are called Christ-ians. I have traveled extensively. I have suffered hunger, beatings, imprisonments, and threats of death. All this I do gladly for the sake of Jesus who died for me—for the One who forgave me. I am currently in a Roman prison and am condemned to die, which I willingly do for the One who died for me.

Mary

Mary (Sister of Martha and Lazarus)

My name is Mary. Right now the name Mary is very popular, and I know of several women by this name. Sometimes we are distinguished by who our families are or where we live. My home is in Bethany, near Jerusalem with my sister and brother. Martha, Lazarus, and I live in the house that Lazarus naturally inherited after our parents died. It is comfortable and large enough for dinner and houseguests.

Lazarus and some of our relatives hold high positions of authority in Jerusalem. He is well-respected by all who know him. Being our big brother, Martha and I love him dearly. He was, however, always prone to illness and weakness, so Martha made sure he ate well. Always admonishing, "Lazarus, dear, you need more meat to cover your bones. They are sticking out like a baby goat's." She watched over him like a mother hen.

Mother hen. I guess that was Martha's self-appointed role in our household—one of them! She fussed *over* Lazarus and she fussed *at* me. Fussed and controlled! She was always "in charge" and could "take charge" of almost anything. She was skilled, organized, and busy all the time.

I lacked all the domestic talents that Martha had—the abilities she continually tried to instill in me. It was exhausting to both Martha and me, to inspire hard work into a dreamer, as she called me. I called her inflexible. I much preferred wandering among the street vendors, seeing the colorful fabrics and trinkets, tasting exotic foods, and meeting people.

One day, while in town, I caught the eye of a handsome man looking at me. We both smiled. After looking around at the crowd, he cautiously walked over to me. As he got closer, I noticed he was extremely well-dressed. *Oh no—he's a Pharisee! Is he coming to reprimand me for my dress or my flirtatious behavior?*

"Hello, young lady. My name is Simon."

"I am Mary. My brother is Lazarus—perhaps you know him?" We exchanged a few pleasantries, and I told him I was coming back tomorrow to purchase the colorful fabric that had caught my eye. He nodded, smiled, and we parted.

The next day, I returned to the market place, hoping to see this handsome man again. There he was. Simon had purchased the very expensive fabric I had admired the day before and gave it to me. Wonderful! Not only did I get my fabric, but I also got the attention of a distinguished man. More small talk that led to sweet looks and words, that led to…

Our secret affair lasted a few short weeks. My dreams were high and life was exciting! Then suddenly, he wanted nothing more to do with me. What did I do to cause him to reject me now? I pleaded, I begged, I humiliated myself! Now I was discarded and cast aside like something dirty. Out on the streets! I couldn't bear his rejection and needed to leave town. Leave Bethany!

I moved to the small town of Magdala, in the region of Galilee, west of the Sea.

My roommate and I decided to set up a fortune-telling booth at the market place. We were both Jews and knew the laws of Moses and the prophets forbidding such practices, but this wasn't *real.* It was just for fun! We pretended to look into someone's future by using various objects, gadgets, and gyrations. We became a popular attraction and made enough money to pay the landlord, plus extra, for more seductive clothes and jewels.

Curiously, my fortune-telling was not only lucrative but becoming quite accurate, and in some cases, dead-on. I thought I had a genuine skill for this. Now I was making *lots* of money. But, after a short time, I started suffering from insomnia, with tossing and turning. I heard voices at night! Voices telling me exciting and yet terrible things! I became obsessed, manic, and frenzied, and cared less about my appearance. I lost weight and the natural color in my face. I needed more and more makeup, jewelry, and seductive clothes to attract attention and customers.

I knew my life was immoral and sinful according to Jewish law, but I had no *desire* or *power* to change it. "Desire?" Maybe a trifle. "Power?" No! I had no control. I was *controlled!* Controlled by something strong and commanding! Demons?

One day a man came to my village. I don't know why, but I ran to Him and fell at His feet, screaming terrible and vile things until I was weak and totally exhausted. Finally, a few whispered words escaped my lips, "Help me. Please help me." He bent down and pulled my tangled hair from my face and looked directly into my eyes. At first, His eyes looked at me with compassion and love. Then His eyes seemed to be filled with anger. Anger and power! Looking up into the heavens, He said something—something I didn't understand.

Then the violence began! Vile shouting, convulsing, flailing, spitting, laughing, spasms, and growling like a rabid dog. Seven repulsive behaviors by seven foul demons controlling my body. When this ferocity was finally over, I was weak as a kitten, weak as a newborn baby. All my strength was gone, and I lay in a dusty heap. Someone from the crowd asked, "Is she dead?" When I looked up, the only One near me was that same man who was looking into my eyes and smiling. All others of the crowd had backed clear of my actions. Now, my only desire was to know this man. *Who is He? What is this power He demonstrated over me and the demons inside of me? Will He let me follow him?*

After washing my face, removing the filthy and seductive clothes, cleaning my matted and dirty hair, I looked for the man who saved and changed my life. And I joined the crowd that seemed to be with Him. I, too, wanted to be close and hear His voice, and more words of promise and comfort.

I traveled with Jesus and His disciples back to my home in Bethany. I wasn't sure how Martha and Lazarus would react toward me. They were *surprised* but welcomed me with open arms and hearts and accepted the change in my life. They invited Jesus and His disciples to stay awhile, to rest and visit. And, of course, have a good meal prepared by Martha! Lazarus and I loved listening to Jesus. Martha did too, but was busy, as always, being the perfect hostess. Sometimes, along with other women, I traveled with Jesus and His disciples. I saw many marvelous things.

Perhaps the most powerful miracles, in my eyes, are casting out the demons. It is such a personal miracle for me. I have a unique testimony!

My brother, Lazarus, was not a strong man. He always did what he could around our house but often needed rest, more and more rest lately. Eventually, he got a very high fever that Martha and the doctors could not break. Knowing the healing that Jesus had done for strangers, Martha was sure He would heal a friend. She sent for Jesus!

But, soon after, Lazarus died. What a heartbreak! Devastating! Washing and wrapping his body for burial was crushing. Martha kept whispering, "Where is Jesus? Where was He when Lazarus needed Him most?"

Four days later, after Lazarus was buried, Martha got word that Jesus was on His way. She ran to meet Him. I stayed behind, not wanting to see anyone. But a message was sent that Jesus was calling for *me.* At the tomb, Jesus was crying. Yes, Jesus loved Lazarus too. After wiping His tears, He ordered the huge stone covering the tomb to be rolled away. Everyone gasped! After four days, a dead body would have a terrible smell, especially in this Judaean heat! Holding His arms up, Jesus shouted, "Lazarus, come out!" *I often wondered if Jesus hadn't called Lazarus by name, would the power of His words cause other bodies to come out too?*

Suddenly, there stood Lazarus still wrapped in burial cloths. Jesus told us to unwrap his body and give him clothes to wear. Now our tears of sadness turned to tears of unspeakable joy and thanksgiving.

Shortly after that, Simon the Pharisee (the man of my sinful past), who had been healed of leprosy by Jesus, arranged for a large dinner celebration with many friends. Jesus was the guest of honor. Naturally, Martha was the hostess. She loved the preparations, the challenge. And she loved Jesus, the honored guest. I helped Martha before the guests arrived, but when I saw Jesus, my heart went out to Him, and I wanted to do something special for my Lord. He had spoken several times about His own death, which was most difficult to hear. I suddenly remembered the sealed box of burial perfume I had purchased in anticipation of this tragic occasion. It was very expensive—the best I could buy.

I ran home to get the box. It was my thank-offering to Jesus for saving my life. With trembling hands, I wanted to offer it to Him now, before

His death. *How should I do this? Do I give the box to Jesus? Do I wait until His death? Do I anoint Him now?*

It was early evening, and the banquet room had an inviting warm glow with hanging oil lamps. The guests were comfortable and reclining at the table laden with exquisite food. My brother, Lazarus, was next to Jesus. With my throat tightened and tears obscuring my vision, and without a thought for anyone except Jesus, I knelt at His feet. In the shadows of this room, I broke the box and poured its rich and powerful smelling oil over His feet and head. My emotions were so strong, I couldn't speak—just my tears, mingled with the fragrance, spilled over His body. I vaguely heard some murmuring and complaining over what I had done. I felt embarrassed, but not ashamed. The only words I heard clearly were expressions of compassion coming from Jesus. I know Jesus loves me and has forgiven me of my past.

The following days of the Jewish Passover were a whirlwind of activity in Jerusalem. People came from all over, some traveling for days or weeks. They crowded the streets, the inns, and the hillsides. It should have been a peaceful and holy celebration. But it seemed chaotic, with outbreaks, complaining, fighting, shoving, and corruption by the temple money changers. People brought their "perfect lambs" for sacrificing, which were often rejected as "imperfect" by the Pharisees or money changers, then were sold another lamb at a very high price.

During all this disorder and chaos, it was hard to stay close to Jesus and his disciples. I did, however, witness Jesus riding into Jerusalem on a donkey. People waved palm branches and hailed Him, "King of the Jews." What a thrill! How exciting! Yes!

On Friday of the Passover, I heard that Jesus was on trial. Trial for treason. Trial for His life. How could this be? Just a few days before, He was hailed "King of the Jews." *Surely, God won't allow Jesus to be executed? Die at the hands of the Romans—and for treason!*

I got to Jerusalem just in time to see Jesus' weak and bleeding body struggling to carry His own cross to be *crucified*. It was obvious He had suffered immense cruelty. Yes, Jesus had foretold of His death, but to be tortured and crucified by Rome? Where did this come from? How did this happen? Who was behind all this? Crucified?

I found only one of Jesus' disciples, John, who was with the mother of my precious Master. Where were His other disciples? Where were His friends? I stayed with John and Mary at the cross. That bitter, cruel, implement of Roman torture and death. Our hopes crushed! Our hearts broken! Our future gone!

After Jesus died, I helped prepare Him for burial by washing and wrapping His precious body. Where was my sweet-smelling oil *now?* I could have used it *now* to prepare Him for burial. I regretted not having it but was glad I had offered my gift while He was still *alive* to show my love and appreciation to Him.

Over the Sabbath, I never left my room or my tear-soaked pillow. The next day, while it was still dark, I went to the tomb to anoint His body with borrowed ointment and found the tomb empty! *Now what? Isn't crucifying Him enough? Do they have to desecrate His body more? Perhaps His friends have moved Him? But where?*

I ran to where I thought the disciples might be. I told them, "Jesus' body is gone. I don't know where!" Pushing me out of the way, Peter and John ran out the door. I followed but could not keep up with them. It was still quite dark when I arrived again at the tomb.

While crying alone in the dark, I saw a faint movement off to my side. I called to the gardener, "Sir, I came to anoint my friend in His tomb, but He is gone. Do you know where they have taken Him?"

The gardener's only word was, "Mary." I recognized this voice! The voice of my Master! I ran to Him and fell at His feet and reached out to Him. In His most precious and loving voice, He told me, "Mary, don't hold onto me. I must first go to my Father in Heaven. Go and tell Peter I am alive! I will see everyone soon."

I didn't want to let go of Jesus' feet, but I did what He told me to do. I ran back to the room and told Peter and the others that Jesus was alive! Alive! Of course, they didn't believe me! They just dismissed me as being hysterical and foolish. What could I do to *prove* it? Nothing! Not until Jesus appeared to them personally did they believe.

Over the next month or so, I saw Jesus many times. I always felt Jesus was the Messiah, but now I *know* He is the Son of God. And I will someday see Him again in His kingdom of heaven and sitting beside the Father.

Has my life changed since knowing Jesus? Undoubtedly, yes! From a selfish, immature, and demon-possessed woman to a forgiven child of God. I do what I can to spread the good news about Jesus and His saving power. I spend much of my time caring for the widows and children. Telling them my story of knowing and loving Jesus gives them hope.

Judas

Judas (The Betrayer)

My name is Judas Iscariot, first son of Simon Iscariot. We are devout Jews and live in a large and comfortable house overlooking a beautiful valley. Being orthodox Jews and looking forward to the coming Messiah, my family saw to it that I received a superior education from the rabbis in the synagogue in Jerusalem. I even did some teaching of a few young boys myself. The ancient scriptures prophesied the arrival of our long-awaited Messiah to break the bonds of Rome. All Jews hated Rome!

While traveling the countryside one day, I came upon a group of people who were gathered around a preacher talking about the kingdom of heaven. He was dressed in simple clothes. His voice was clear, strong, yet tender, and clearly had the full attention of those near Him. He spoke with passion and seemed to have *personal* knowledge and love of the scriptures—those same dry scriptures I had learned about from my teachers and rabbis. I was drawn to Him, but stayed on the outskirts of this company.

A few days later, I looked for Him. Again, He was surrounded by men, women, and children listening to Him, and some were healed of their various illnesses. He was definitely becoming very popular, and I found myself wanting to be around Him too. His name was Jesus.

Before I spoke directly to Jesus, I questioned one of His followers. "You certainly have great admiration toward this Man. What is your mission? What are your plans?"

"We are with the Messiah!" Then added, "Come and join us."

"The Messiah, huh? Are you sure?" I asked. "The Messiah is going to save us from Rome. This man just looks like a simple preacher. And I heard He is from Nazareth!"

"Come! Come and meet Jesus." Then taking my arm, we walked up to Jesus. I came face to face with kindness, with compassion, and I felt drawn to His inviting spirit.

I asked, "Kind Teacher, may I join You and Your followers? I am also a teacher, and I may be of some value and assistance to Your calling and mission." With kind eyes and a gentle manner, He told me that He and his followers had no permanent place to stay, but traveled from town to village. (He must have said that because I was obviously dressed better than the others and, of course, appeared to have a higher status than these common country folk.) Still, He didn't say I could *not* join Him. Before returning the next day, I had reluctantly removed my more costly clothing. But I needed to dress as the others, so I could blend in better and be accepted and welcomed into their company.

Traveling with Jesus, I saw many wonderful things. When Jesus blessed a young boy's lunch, I, along with the others, handed out the bread and fish to the multitude. What an experience! It was exhilarating to be involved. *I* was praised and thanked for this bread—this simple lunch!

I saw people being healed of terrible diseases, demons cast out, even the dead raised to life. With all these wonderful miracles, I knew Jesus had to have come from God, but could not see how *He* could possibly be the promised Messiah. He didn't possess the political clout to overthrow Rome. And He didn't have the powerful Jewish leaders on his side. Sometimes, He even seemed to alienate them and their authority. Why?

Jesus was gaining more and more popularity and drew people from all over to hear Him and to be healed of their diseases. With His popularity and with *my* connections, *my* intelligence, and *my* contributions, I could advance His purpose and set Him up as King of the Jews—Messiah or not. Undoubtedly, I would then be given a high position in this new kingdom. Jesus just needed help—*my* help!

It bothered me that Jesus talked often of trials and persecution for Himself, and that His kingdom was *not* of this world, but of a "Heavenly Kingdom" and the "Kingdom of God." *If Jesus is the Messiah, isn't He supposed to sit on David's throne?* I grew increasingly disappointed in the progression of this new movement. I began to back away emotionally from the others but was still considered part of the *inner circle*. The disciples seemed to hold me in high regard and sometimes sought my opinion. And I carried the purse, meager as it was! Who would know if I occasionally used some of it for myself?

The major turning point of my respect and loyalty to Jesus was at a dinner held by a wealthy Pharisee named Simon. To show his thankfulness to Jesus for his being healed of leprosy, Simon gave a large banquet in Jesus' honor. Lazarus, who had been raised to life, was there, along with other influential people. I was among the distinguished guests. Martha, known for her excellent meals and beautiful decor, prepared the feast.

During the meal, a powerful fragrance filled the room. An extremely expensive bottle of alabaster had been opened and poured over the head and feet of Jesus. This woman was crying and wiping Jesus' feet with her hair. *How can she humiliate herself like this?* All was quiet, until I mentioned the *cost* of this perfume. Saying with disgust, "What a waste! This could easily have been sold for a lot of money. We could add it to the purse and the money used to feed the poor!" (Not that I really cared about the *poor*, but a little extra money in the purse would feel nice! Very nice!)

Then the rebuke! The rebuke to *me*—not to her! She was obviously a sinful woman and expressed her compassion and gratitude to Jesus openly. Openly! How humiliating! How degrading! A few people looked at me to see my response to this rebuke, but I concealed my wounded pride and my desire for revenge. The time had come for action! No longer would I sit back and play the passive follower, believer, or servant. *Servant—I hate that word, especially if it applies to* me*!*

A day or two later, while I was still rankling over the reproach, I met an important-looking man. Well-dressed, well-spoken, and sympathetic to my frustrations. We talked, and he seemed to understand my annoyance and dissatisfaction. He said his name was Abaddon. Somehow, that name rang a sour note with me, but I immediately brushed it off. We talked for hours.

Abaddon mentioned that I would be wise to consider *forcing* the hand of Jesus. "The Pharisees hate Jesus and are jealous of His popularity with the people. Since Jesus claims to be the Son of God, they are accusing Him of blasphemy, which is punishable by death by *our* laws. If Jesus can be arrested by the Pharisees, He may be *forced* to claim His right to David's throne. Or they could have Him executed. In either case, don't worry! If the death of Jesus is in God's plan, it won't be *your fault.*" Then he added, "Be sure His arrest is done at night and in seclusion, when there would be less uprising from the people." My friendship with Abaddon was also in secret, usually at night or in hidden quarters. He was compelling, mesmerizing, and virtually irresistible.

Soon, I secretly met with Caiaphas, the High Priest. Tentative plans were laid until the opportune moment presented itself. We dickered over the bounty, but finally agreed on thirty pieces of silver—the price of a slave! I, of course, desired more, but consented to his proposed price. I could have made a lot more money if I had been able to get my hands on that alabaster box! Now I had to wait and look for the perfect moment. Hidden moment. Safe from His adoring crowds.

It was Passover time, and the Passover meal was ready for us in an upper room. I always enjoyed this yearly event, but that night, my mind was elsewhere. Since there was no servant to wash our feet, everyone looked around. It was uncomfortable, but in no way was I willing to wash the feet of these simple men—or *any* feet, for that matter.

A hush fell over the room as Jesus arose from the table. He walked over to the filled basin of water, removed the towel from the peg on the wall, and prepared Himself to wash our feet. He came to me first. *Me first!* I have to admit, my reaction was twofold—pride and shame. With tenderness, Jesus washed my feet and looked longingly into my eyes. I was torn! Conflicted! I came close, *too close*, to confessing my actions; and I might have, if it weren't for the others watching me closely. I couldn't appear weak! Not now!

During our meal, Jesus announced that one of us was going to betray Him. Every man there asked Him, "Is it I?" Not wanting to appear indifferent to Jesus' troubled countenance, I also inquired if I was the betrayer.

Jesus solemnly replied, "As you have said! Now what you are planning to do, do it quickly." *Does Jesus know? Does He really know?* No matter, my mind was made up. It was the point of no return!

When I got downstairs to the street, Abaddon was waiting for me, encouraging me. (It was comforting to have a *friend* who understood me, yet somehow unsettling!) We hurried to Caiaphas's palace, but Abaddon stayed outside. I gave Caiaphas the information that I was sure Jesus would soon be in the Garden of Gethsemane with His followers. "In the darkness, your police might try to arrest the wrong man. Therefore, I will lead the men, and I will rush toward Jesus and kiss Him in apparent sympathy. It is extremely important that you bind His hands tightly and securely." I stressed the importance of binding His hands firmly because I didn't want to be blamed if Jesus evaded their arrest.

Then I got paid! Paid for my vision, my cunning, my treachery, my betrayal. Yes, I got my thirty pieces of silver. Very dramatically, Caiaphas let each coin drop separately into my opened hands and counted them out slowly. He let the sound of each silver coin echo in the judgment hall. I had as much contempt for him as he had for me. But no matter!

The temple police, the priests, the soldiers, and the night "cockroaches" were very noisy as we approached the garden. I ran up to Jesus who was standing poised and dignified, and I kissed Him. Jesus said, "Friend, did you come to betray the Son of Man with a kiss?"

"Friend?" He called me *friend!* Didn't Jesus know what was *really* happening while the soldiers were quickly binding His hands?

There was a brief skirmish and confusion with swords, screaming, and a bloodied ear. The strong cords fell off of Jesus' hands, and He replaced and healed the ear of Malchus, the High Priest's servant. Then Jesus was *again* shackled, and roughly taken to Annas, the ex-High Priest and father-in-law of Caiaphas. (Annas had been removed from his position as High Priest by the Governor Gratus for his executing capital punishments, which was forbidden by Rome. Still, Annas wielded a lot influence and power over the Jews and the Sanhedrin.)

I walked beside Jesus while the others, His *true* friends ran. Ran like rats. Frightened and hiding! *So I am not the only one who is betraying Jesus. Those who promised to stay by Him and even die for Him are now cowards! They are scattering like sheep in the presence of wolves!*

During the three years I had spent with Jesus and His disciples, I knew Him to be a good man, a man of God—someone who, with His popularity and *my assistance,* could become powerful enough to weaken the power of Rome and sit on the Throne of David—with *me* beside Him. However, I was never truly convinced that Jesus was the Messiah, the Son of God.

The next trial was by Caiaphas, the High Priest. It was a farce! Abaddon was now standing beside me and said with a sinister attitude, "This will give Jesus the perfect opportunity to reveal Himself as the Son of God! To uncloak His Divinity! To prove His Deity! To save Himself!" I was confused. Abaddon sounded as if he *knew* Jesus was who He claimed to be.

During the "trial," Jesus was calm and answered questions with poise and dignity amid flying accusations and false testimonies. Everything was going wrong. Wrong! My plans had failed. Now I hated Caiaphas. I hated myself. And I even hated the man who was sentenced by Jewish law to be killed for blasphemy. Additional charges of sedition against Rome were made to insure His condemnation and execution. The illegal trial was basically over!

Now, wracked with tremendous guilt and with the thirty pieces of silver clutched tightly in my hand, I ran to Caiaphas and threw the silver *at* him. Once again, the sound of money echoed in the hall. I yelled, "This man is innocent and not worthy of death!" It seemed every eye was looking at me, but not for the reasons I desired. Then, confessing, I cried, "I have sinned. I have betrayed innocent blood!"

Caiaphas looked angry. Glancing around the judgment hall, he realized everyone knew of his contribution to the betrayal and the thirty pieces of silver! After regaining his composure, he said with an indifferent wave of his hand, "What is that to us?" All was quiet except for a muffled snicker from my friend, Abaddon.

It was over! Condemned, Jesus was to be taken to Pontius Pilate. In a last-ditch effort to justify myself, I cast my body at Jesus' feet. I begged Him, "Save Yourself. It has gone too far, and there is nothing more I can do! It is too late! Too late! Save Yourself!"

I watched the crowd violently and savagely take Jesus from Caiaphas's judgment hall to Pilate. They needed Rome's approval for their hatred and decisions. Approval for their sentence deserving execution.

I could not witness this any longer. I looked for Abbadon, but apparently, he had gone with the mob. I was alone, all alone! Alone with only my thoughts and my guilt!

Has my life changed after knowing Jesus? I had a life of riches and fine clothes before knowing Jesus. I was well educated and I had ambition. High ambition that failed! For three years, I lived hand-to-mouth, wore clothes and sandals of the poor, and longed for riches and honor. My plans, my aspirations, my elevated position in the new Kingdom, failed. And I cannot continue to face this failure. It was my sin that stabbed my heart, but it was my guilt that twisted the blade! So you ask me if my life has changed while I am standing under this dead tree and holding this rope?

Centurian

The Centurion

My name is Druses, and it was only natural for me to become a Roman soldier. My father was a centurion and well respected among other centurions and leaders in the powerful Roman military. He fought in many wars and was killed defending the Empire. A soldier's death! An honorable death!

Augustus (originally named Octavian and grandnephew of Julius Caesar) was the emperor when I was a young boy. He instigated progressive changes to stabilize and strengthen the government. He made a tax system that was more fair, and he ordered a census of the entire empire. It became a time of peace and prosperity. New roads, forts, and aqueducts were built by slaves. My older brothers and I went to school and were taught to read and write as were all citizens in Rome. The many slaves, however, were not given this privilege.

The Roman Empire extended from Britain in the West to Mesopotamia in the East. It surrounded the Mediterranean with its many trade routes and seaports. The empire included a vast number of people with their own cultures, languages, and religious beliefs. This was tolerated as long as they paid their taxes. Any uprisings could easily be suppressed by the strength of Rome.

We have many gods. Our gods were adopted from the Greek culture—just given different names. These gods are powerful and sometimes cruel to those who displeased them. The gods (and no one knows how many there are) are greatly feared!

When my brothers and I became of age, we joined the Roman army. This was expected, so we didn't have a lot of choice. I was strong and learned quickly how to fight. We practiced fighting each other in training and even fought with the gladiators. Besides being skilled with swords and the many other implements of war, we were taught loyalty, courage, and respect for authority. Our instruction was mixed with rewards and harsh punishments. Our courage was honored with praises and gifts.

After a few years of strenuously hard work as a foot soldier, I was promoted to the title of centurion. It was a very proud day, earning the same military position as my father. Now I was in charge of one hundred men and could ride a horse. My uniform changed to indicate my higher status, and I chose to wear the helmet of my father.

Judaea was an area east of the Mediterranean and north of Egypt. It was always an area of civil unrest and resistance to Rome by the Jewish nation. A shrewd man by the name of Herod, who was part Jewish himself, took advantage of this rebellion and his friendship with Augustus, and was given the title of King of the Jews in Judaea.

Herod, called "the Great," had massive building projects. He rebuilt and enlarged the Jewish temple in Jerusalem—later called Herod's Temple. Even with this new and beautiful temple, the Jewish zealots remained hostile and resistant and unwilling to live under Roman rule. Fanatical and uncompromising!

After Herod the Great died, one of his sons, Herod Antipas, was named King of the Jews in Jerusalem. Eventually, more Roman power was needed in Judaea, and legions of soldiers were sent to quash the rising unrest and rebellion. The old, weak, and paranoid Tiberius was Caesar in Rome, but living in Capri.

While Herod Antipas was king in Jerusalem, I was sent, along with the one hundred men in my command, to this hot and arid territory. Certainly not my choice, but soldiers are directed wherever needed for the sake of the empire and the glory of Rome. Arriving in Judaea was all that I had dreaded it would be. Hot. Sticky. Inhospitable. We were greeted with suspicion and hostility. But I had the political strength of Tiberius and the Roman Empire behind me. I gave encouragement to my men saying, "Be strong. Don't be intimidated. Report to me any threats of insurrection or sedition."

I learned the Jews were anticipating the coming of a Messiah, a Savior, a *new* King of the Jews. This had been foretold hundreds of years before by their prophets, and the "time was near" for this prophecy to be fulfilled. This caused the Jewish leaders to become bolder in their rebellion against Rome.

There were two men, (both of them Jews) that caused a lot of attention and excitement. One was dressed in a short and simple garment made of camel hair. He lived and preached near the Jordan River and did a lot of shouting about the need for men to change their lives and to look for the coming Messiah. He encouraged them to get into the river with him, where he pushed their heads briefly under the water. He called it "baptism." The whole process was completely foreign and strange to me, but he seemed to be a good man.

The other man traveled from town to town, preaching and healing the sick. *Interesting! Is He really healing these people, or is this some kind of trickery?* I saw lots of "magic" while living in Rome. Magic that put anxiety and apprehension into the people observing the sorcery. This man's "magic" was clean and open, and He didn't ask for money!

This Jew always had a crowd following Him. As far as I could see, there wasn't any real disturbance. I saw nothing that needed my intervention. As a matter of fact, I rather enjoyed listening to Him, but I was not invited to get very near. I was looked upon with suspicion, so I stayed on the outskirts of the crowd. I was surprised and pleased one day, when I heard the man tell the Jewish leaders that they are obliged to pay their taxes to Caesar, or something like that. It didn't sound to me like He was inciting a revolution against the empire. *Why is this man someone I need to watch for crimes against Rome?*

Matius, who was also a centurion, became a friend of mine. He had lived in Judaea with his family for many years. While visiting him, I saw that one of his servants was very ill. It appeared he was in a lot of pain and close to death. Matius had done everything he knew to help his servant. Finally, he said, "I know of a Jewish healer by the name of Jesus. Let's find Him, and I will ask Him for healing."

"Matius, he is a *Jew*, and we are *Romans!* He won't help you. The Jews hate us!"

"I know, Druses, I know. But He is a *good* man, and I believe the stories I've heard about Him. I have confidence He will fulfill my request."

We eventually found this Jesus among a crowd of people. That didn't stop my friend. He walked right up to Jesus and explained the dire situation of his trusted servant and asked for healing.

Jesus said He would go with Matius and heal the servant, but Matius stopped Him, saying, "Please, I am not worthy to have You come to my house. Just speak the word only and my servant will be healed." (Matius and I both knew about speaking orders. Being Roman centurions, we could command, and orders would be obeyed!)

I had witnessed some of Jesus' "healings." He always put His hands somewhere on the petitioner. But speaking the word *only?* I was sure this was beyond even *His* powers. When we returned to Matius's house, the servant was awake, well, and serving others. Amazing! Unbelievable! *Who is this Jesus?*

Which god did this healing? I believe in and fear many gods. The Jews say they believe in only one God. I don't understand! Is this Jesus a God?

Many Jews from all over and faraway places come to Jerusalem once a year for a festival. It is very crowded and generally peaceful. An occasional skirmish erupts, but nothing very serious. This year, however, excitement escalated when this Jesus was riding on a donkey and traveling toward the city of Jerusalem. The crowds waved palm branches and placed their garments on the ground for the donkey to walk on. Apparently, the people were accepting Jesus as a king. A king? This enthusiastic demonstration could certainly be considered rebellious and subversive.

When Jesus got to the temple, there was chaos. Chaos and noise! Noise from people buying, selling, yelling! Noise of coins falling into the hands of the money exchangers, and the temple tax collectors! Noise from coins falling on the stone floor! And animals! Sheep and birds were everywhere!

I could see the disgust in the eyes of Jesus. (I was watching Him closely.) He took a braided cord and started swinging it around. He rushed over to the tables and overturned them. The money flew everywhere. He accused the people of turning *His* Father's house into a market place, a house of thieves and whores, or something like that. People ran, animals escaped, but the children began to gather around Him.

It seemed like something was about to happen in Jerusalem. Something big. Something I could not stop. Something to do with this Jesus. *Should I stop this? Can I stop this? Do I want to stop it?*

Just a few days later, I was ordered to follow some of the Jewish leaders to arrest a man who was undermining the Jewish traditions. I was told He was the one who was subversive and causing a revolution. Another Jewish malcontent! Maybe this whole threat to the empire could finally be stopped. Finished! Finally finished!

It was quite late at night, so I and a few of my men with lanterns, followed some of the frenzied Jewish leaders to an olive grove and garden. They were making so much noise! I thought any person or troublemaker, would surely leave quickly and escape an arrest or capture.

Upon our arrival, there was this *Jesus!* Was He the *troublemaker?* The *revolutionary?* He was standing poised and unperturbed, and asked who we were looking for. The leader of the entourage ran up and kissed Jesus repeatedly on the cheek, and looked as if he were crying in sympathy. That didn't make sense to me. If he was among *our* group, why did he act like he was a friend of Jesus? He obviously knew Him.

Jesus calmly admitted that He was the one we were looking for, but requested that His friends be free to leave. After His hands were tied behind His back, one of His friends (the only one left) drew his long knife and cut off the ear of Malchus, the High Priest's servant. Then there was shoving and pushing, yelling and shouting, and screaming from the man with the missing ear!

Before a full riot broke out, the cords that tied Jesus' hands fell to the ground, and He put the ear back on the terrified and bleeding man. Completely restored! The only evidence was the blood still on his neck and clothes. Now that his ear was healed, Malchus backed away to the edge of the crowd. Quiet and subdued. One of my soldiers then stepped forward and reapplied the shackles. Even though Jesus offered no resistance, He was brutally treated. Shoved, kicked, and hit with sticks.

I don't understand these Jews! Every day, in open daylight, Jesus was among them, doing His teaching and healing. Why didn't they arrest Him in the light of day? Why did they wait to arrest Him in the cloak of darkness and secrecy? What were they afraid of? Why were they treating a lamb like a lion?

Jesus was taken to a couple of the Jewish high priests to be judged by their laws. With reddened faces contorted with passion, the priests accused the composed and bound prisoner before them of blasphemy—worthy of death by Jewish law. Of course, Roman law would not condone a death because of blasphemy, and they knew it! Still, Jesus was condemned to death by this *farce* of a trial. When His sentence was announced, the rabble in attendance rushed toward Him. He had previously been brutally beaten, but if it hadn't been for my soldiers, they would have killed this man.

Because the Jewish leaders needed the consent of Rome to kill Jesus, they took Him early that same morning to Pilate, the Roman Governor. Irritated at such a request for a hasty decision, Pilate appeared impatient. The Jewish leaders had not lessened their fury or their appetite for *blood* against the composed and dignified prisoner standing before them. The contrast was obvious and tremendously striking! Peace versus violence!

Pilate had a hard time getting a straight answer to his question. "What has this man done, and why have you brought Him to me?" Their accusations were vague and not worthy of death by Roman law. Finally, they accused Jesus of perverting Rome and refusing to pay taxes to Caesar. This I *knew* was false!

It looked to me like Pilate did not want to condemn this prisoner standing poised before him. He also seemed afraid of the Jews demanding the pronouncement of death. But when he heard of possible subversion to Rome, he quickly jumped at the chance to transfer the *problem* to King Herod, who was in Jerusalem at the time.

I had never previously seen Herod, so I was excited and pleased to accompany the prisoner to the king. What a disappointment! Whereas Pilate was weak and vacillating, Herod was vain and pompous! After not getting any response from Jesus—either by threats or promises—he had Jesus beaten, then draped a dirty royal robe on Him. Again, Jesus had no words for Herod, which seemed to frustrate and infuriate him. Then, demonstrating his cruelty and indifference to justice, and hoping to satisfy the Jewish dignitaries, he had Jesus scourged another time before sending Him back to Pilate. This time, one of my soldiers twisted some branches of a thorn bush and made a crown. A crown of thorns! "A crown for the King!" they shouted as they made a mockery of bowing to Him.

How much can this man take? Will no one come to His defense? I am a proud soldier of Rome, yet this is making me sick. I have contributed to the suffering of criminals. Justified punishment! But this...

Back in Pilate's judgment hall, I stood behind Pilate and off to the side. I stood far enough away to not interfere with the proceedings, yet visible enough to demonstrate control and influence. Suddenly, Pilate's wife gave me a note to be passed to her husband. Pilate quickly read the note. He paled and appeared shaken. Their eyes connected for several moments then he nodded slightly to her. His head was down as if in deep thought. Then he turned to me and told me to bring out another condemned prisoner, "Bring out Barabbas."

Barabbas was a dangerous and violent convict who was condemned to death. I, and three of my soldiers, brought him up from the dungeon in heavy chains. He shouted and swore, and spit at Pilate and the mob. One soldier hit him hard, but that made no difference.

Pilate then offered the Jews a choice—to free the murderer Barabbas, or the man called Jesus. I didn't understand what was going on. Why was Pilate doing that? Why would he offer to free such a treacherous savage? I then realized it was Pilate's way of avoiding the demands of the mob. He stood them side by side—the contrast was unmistakable. Beast and Beauty. Brutal and Benevolent. Lion and Lamb. Demon and Divine.

Here was now a *chance* to bring an end to the injustice toward Jesus. But the mob yelled, "Barabbas, Barabbas, give us Barabbas." Pilate looked around to me, frowning. He must have thought the unruly rabble before him misunderstood the offer because he asked again, "Do you want me to release to you your king?"

"No," they shouted. "We have no king but Caesar! Give us Barabbas!" Unbelievable! Even some of my soldiers were softening their opinion toward this Jesus and directing their hostile attitude toward the vicious horde that seemed devil possessed.

"What shall I do with this man called Jesus?"

"Crucify him! Crucify him!"

Pilate then ordered a basin of water and a towel brought to him. He ceremoniously washed his hands before the briefly quieted mob. After drying his hands, he threw down the towel in apparent disgust. Walking over to Jesus, he placed a hand on His bruised and bleeding shoulder, and said, "I find no fault in this man. Here is your king. Behold the man! Do with Him as you wish. My hands are clean. His blood is on you!"

Again, a tremendous uproar! "His blood is on us and our children!"

Pilate nodded to me. My unspoken orders were given. I felt sick to my stomach! As I looked around to the soldiers, some would not even look at me, others were ready and eager for their Roman duty. As was my practice before such horrifying missions, I gave my men cheap wine to dull their senses. Harden their hearts! Strengthen their commitment!

Death by crucifixion is extremely cruel, slow, and an ignominious way to die. It was reserved for the most vile of criminals. Certainly not for this Jesus! By the time this whole façade of justice was over and we were on our way to Golgotha (the place of crucifixions), it was early afternoon.

As was the custom, prisoners were forced to carry their own implement of torture and death. Being very weak from several absurd court trials with no rest, no food or water, and multiple beatings during the last couple of days, Jesus fell under the load of the heavy cross. I was tired too, but I was only a *witness* to all this. I could easily *see* His physical suffering but could only *imagine* His mental torment.

One of my soldiers grabbed a man from the crowd and forced him to carry the cross for this weakened and condemned man. He lifted the cross from His back and helped Him to His feet. "Thank you," was Jesus' quiet response. *Thank you?* Even in His humiliation and pain, He expressed appreciation to a stranger?

Upon arrival to the barren rock of death, Jesus was roughly thrown on to the cross lying on the ground. Soldiers slung ropes around His legs and arms—they knew this procedure well. (It was not my job to do the barbaric deed but to oversee the action and maintain crowd control.) Then large spikes were driven through His hands and feet. Jesus offered no resistance. None! Just moans of pain came from His parched lips.

Usually, crucifixions draw only a few spectators, and of course, family members, if there are any. This one, however, attracted a large crowd, which was mostly the same mob in Pilate's court. Instead of just being *satisfied* with their demanded death sentence, they continued to mock and ridicule Jesus. Scorning! Scoffing! Sneering!

In the distance and outskirts of the crowd, I saw many people crying or with heads bowed. Surely, Jesus had *some* friends. But where were they during His trials and His demeaning death?

My own contempt for these Jews was growing by the minute, but what could I do, a soldier of Rome—a centurion? Even if there was *something* I could do, it was too late now. Too late to speak up. Too late to offer comfort. Too late to express my regrets. Too late to save Him.

Even in His misery, Jesus asked His God to "forgive them," adding "For they don't know what they are doing." *What does He mean we don't know?* Regrettably, we had done this many times, and we performed our responsibilities efficiently as directed by Rome.

Or, "*Forgive* them!" Could *I* ever be forgiven? How? If I prayed to one of *my* gods, would I be forgiven for this injustice? Would they hear me? Would they care? Or, if I prayed to the God that Jesus talked to, would *He* hear me, and would *He* care? My head was spinning, and my heart was breaking. I wanted to leave, yet I wanted to stay. Why?

On the other hand, could, "Forgive *them*" mean the Jews? These Jews who were calling for Jesus to perform a miracle for them? Such disrespect! Such contempt! They were unsatisfied with His execution alone—*now* they made fun of Him. Laughed at Him! *How do you laugh at a tortured and dying man?* Cruel and calloused! They reminded me of hungry lions and jackals. Can *they* be forgiven?

A woman, who was shedding bitter tears, slowly approached the cross. She tenderly reached up and touched the bleeding feet of Jesus. I assumed she was His mother. What a sight! She was supported by a young man by her side. Even in His agony, He spoke kindly toward her, and asked the man to take care of her. *Amazing! Who is this man?*

It was early in the afternoon, and an intense darkness settled all around. The sun that had previously been bright and making the day unbearably hot seemed to disappear in the sky. An eerie darkness, a threatening darkness—an omen! Along with this black augur, terrifying groans came from the mob. Frightful! Then lightning all around! Lightning illuminated the dark sky, split trees, and set them on fire. Lightning hit houses, rocks, and opened old graves. An earthquake rolled boulders down hills and mountains. Above this tremendous noise was the screaming of the people and what seemed to be the bellowing of the gods. (Roman gods or the one God of Jesus?) In any case, it seemed that all creation was in rebellion and recoiling at this horrendous event. Some of the mob ran away—ran for their lives—pulling their hair, tearing their clothes, and howling in terror.

After several hours, there was a sudden and clear cry from the One hanging between heaven and hell. "It is finished!" Surprised, I looked closely at Jesus. His head hung forward and He appeared to be dead! Yes, it was indeed finished—finished for Him. He was dead! Somehow, it gave me a sense of relief for the man nailed to the center cross. This Jesus, with a sign above His head testifying to everyone, King of the Jews. No more suffering. No more ridiculing. No more humiliation.

"Surely, this was an innocent and a righteous man! The Son of God!"

A few of His friends came and gently removed Jesus from His cross. Amidst their tears, they treated His body with the utmost respect and tenderness and carried Him someplace to be buried.

My duties, however, were not quite finished. But because the rest of the treacherous mob had scattered like rats, I would soon be able to leave. The other two criminals would eventually die. Eventually! Alone and abandoned! As I was getting ready to leave this tragic event, I received a message:

> You are to break the legs of the other two criminals and remove them from their crosses. The Jewish religious leaders don't want the crucified bodies hanging from crosses on their Holy Sabbath.

They have to be kidding! Those cruel, bloodthirsty Jews celebrate Holy days? Even after the death of the One they hated, they were making more demands of Pilate. After reading the note, I tore it in half, threw it to the ground, and walked away, saying, "Someone else will have to do this." I had lost all respect for Rome. *May the gods forgive me!* I went home. Home to sleep, hopefully *without* dreaming!

The next few days were filled with more threats, confusion, suspicion, and wild stories. There was even a rumor that Jesus was alive! Among the regiment of soldiers assigned to guard the tomb, two of them came to me, telling an unbelievable story, saying, "Sir, we *have* to tell you something! An incredibly bright and strong aberration broke the Roman seal on the tomb and rolled away the stone like it was a *pebble!* Then the dead man came *walking out!* He was alive—*truly alive!* Please, sir, there was *nothing* we could do!" *Can this be true? Are my soldiers lying to me to cover their failure? They know the punishment for negligence. Are the rumors of Jesus being alive really true?* I then remembered thinking that the man who had died on the Roman cross was "the Son of God."

That same Sunday morning of the *supposed* resurrection, I decided to search for some of Jesus' friends, but I couldn't find any. Looking at me suspiciously, someone told me His disciples were in *hiding!* I decided if I removed my centurion uniform, put on the common Jewish clothes, and wore a cap on my head, perhaps I might be given more information. I gave it a try.

A few days later, while still earnestly, but discreetly asking around for the whereabouts of Jesus' followers, a man tapped me on the shoulder. I turned quickly and looked straight into the face of Jesus, the man I had killed! He was smiling, and His eyes were true and forgiving. Here standing before me was the King of the Jews. Not like any king or god I knew. *A true King! A true God!*

I wanted to say something, s*omething* to express my regret for the inhumane treatment and cruelty He received. But I was speechless! Jesus just smiled at me and said, "Go and find Peter. You men have something in common." After telling me how to locate the man named Peter, He turned and walked away. I wanted to follow Him but felt compelled to do as I was told.

When I came across some men by the seaside, I announced, "I am looking for Peter! Is anyone here, Peter, or does anyone know where I can find him?" I was met with fear and suspicion. Looking at me with distrust, they asked, "Who are you? Why are you looking for him?" It took some fast talking, but I finally assured them I wanted to know about Jesus and their God. Adding, "And I was told by Jesus to look for Peter."

Was my life changed? All my life, I wanted to be a centurion like my father. I was so proud of him. A centurion pledges his unquestioning loyalty and obedience to the Roman empire, and my goal was to be promoted to a general. I am not proud of some of my required actions, but I tried, whenever possible, to be humane.

The crucifixion of Jesus was the last one I participated in. In fact, I gave up my commission as a centurion and followed those men who were friends of Jesus, the King of the Jews, and Son of God. I will, no doubt, be executed by Rome as a traitor and a deserter. Until then, I will tell others what I now believe about Jesus.

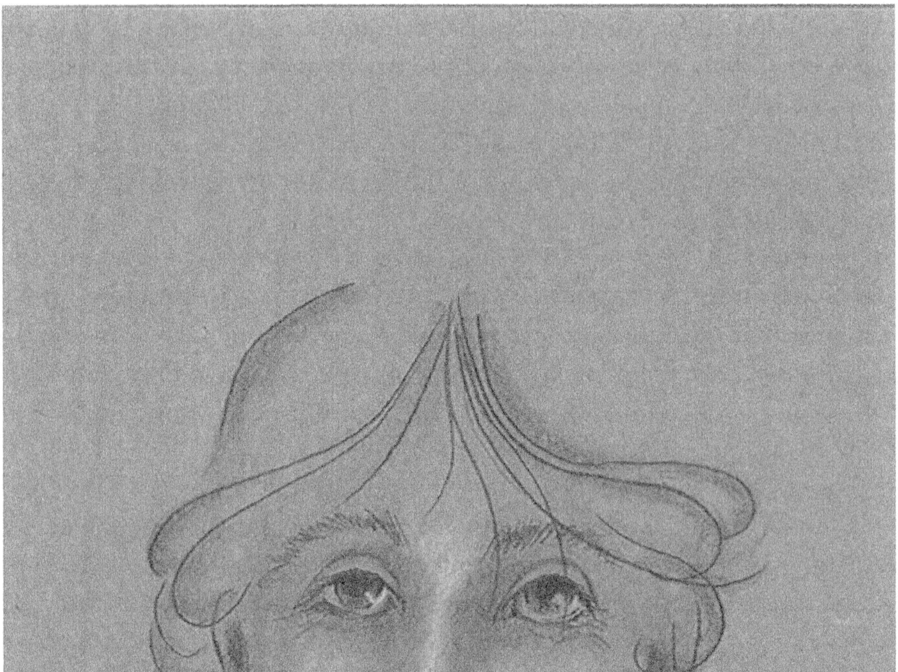
Woman

The Woman at the Well

With tears running down my cheeks and a baby growing in my belly, my parents took John and me to the temple on Mount Gerizim to be married. Mama was crying too, but Papa was angry. Madder than I had ever seen him! We were much too young to be married and had no place to live except with my parents, in a little room in the back of their small house. Papa helped John find a job mending fishnets.

I would say that we were basically happy at first. Like children at play, we felt no responsibility to contribute to the household. We were both immature and selfish in what we expected of each other and my parents. My mother and I fought. John and I fought. My father yelled and threatened.

John became despondent and restless and talked about needing to be free. *Free?*

I realized he had never been around babies, especially *crying* babies. I tried to tell him that things would get better, but I couldn't see any light in our future either.

It wasn't a whole year after our daughter was born when John left. He left me, our daughter, and our childish promises to each other. No word, no, "I'm sorry." He just had few possessions in a rolled-up blanket slung over his shoulder. There were little puffs of dust from his feet as I saw him walking down the road. I was devastated, but if the truth were known, I also envied him. He was *free.* I wasn't.

Sometimes, while my mother babysat, I went to town for some variety and a little excitement in my boring life. After all, I was still very young and needed to have a *life*! One day, I saw a tall and handsome merchant selling a variety of textiles. He didn't notice me at first, so I hurried home to change my clothes, braid my hair, and add some trinkets to my ears, arms, and neck. I was naturally pretty back then, but I wanted extra allurements to catch his attention. It worked!

Every day, I went to town looking for him. His name was Joel, and we became quite interested in each other. He was charming and had a golden voice with compliments to match. He had an exciting life of traveling from village to village and town to town.

I was susceptible to soft and kind words, especially words spoken tenderly by strong men. Words I didn't hear from my father. In asking me to marry him, Joel promised his love "forever and ever" with wine, singing, and dancing.

Before I agreed to marry him, I was hesitant to ask, "What about my daughter, my baby?"

"Sure, bring her along. It will be great, the two of us, I mean the *three* of us. I have plenty of money, and we will show her the world," he promised. Of course, I agreed to marry him! My head and my heart were in the clouds.

Mama tried to talk me out of marrying Joel, and Papa threatened, which he often did. His bellowing could frequently be heard outside our house. He seldom spoke kindly to Mama or me. But I felt like my life was finally going to be really happy. Fulfilling and exciting! Maybe I just needed to get away! My infatuation was blind. My hopes were high and my life now seemed worth living.

It was harder than I had anticipated for those many months. Always traveling! Camping! Keeping up with my husband and the baby who was now more than two years old! Being a charming merchant, Joel caught the eyes of other attractive (and thinner) women. Unreserved flirtatious glances and whispers were shared—just like we had done with each other. I shouldn't have been surprised.

I finally told Joel I was not happy with our lives and especially his actions. He just laughed and said I could leave anytime I wished. He sent me and my daughter packing back home to Samaria. Alone! I felt like my life was over before it barely began. Endless wonder, endless wander!

That was the end of my second marriage but not my humiliation. Papa was angry, of course! Angry at Joel! Angry at me! He reluctantly consented to letting me move back for a short time, until I could find a place of my own, which meant I needed to find a job. Find a job, or find *someone* to support me and my child. Hmm...

How can I weather this storm alone? I need to find someone. Smiling to myself, I thought, *Finding a man will be easier than finding a job!* I guess that is how my young life began to deteriorate further. I knew how to scheme and maneuver. Oh, the slide of compromise. Middle ground. Muddy ground. All in the name of *survival!*

Then later, one of my husbands was killed in a senseless accident caused by the foolishness of his own making. Another husband broke the law and ended up in a Roman prison. I think there were four—no, five husbands in all. There was physical and mental abuse, drunkenness, fighting, yelling, adultery, and abandonment. Men, husbands, beds! Promises made and promises broken! Hearts given and hearts crushed! Dreams imagined and dreams splintered! Doors slammed and doors closed forever. And, of course, two more children with different fathers!

What a mess! The jackals come looking for me. Looking for weakness. Looking for carrion. Hiding does little to protect my children or myself. They find us. Always circling, always looking for a chance to take hurtful bites.

The man who now shares my table and my bed is not my husband, but he is kind. He is much older than my previous husbands and treats my children with indifference, but never hurtful or cruel. He seems to care for me, but does not want to be married. His previous marriages have made him cautious and perhaps bitter. We are quite a pair!

The village I live in is Sychar in Samaria, which is north of Jerusalem. We, who are Jews, have intermarried with the Assyrians and are considered a mixed race and are despised by the Jews, especially those around Jerusalem. They call us half-breeds, corrupt and unworthy to enter their temple, and we are not welcomed in their city. They avoid Samaria while traveling, and they walk *around* it.

Our basic beliefs are the same, but varied in many ways. Our ancestor, Jacob, dug our well and gave it to his son, Joseph. We worship in our temple on Mount Gerizim and are looking for the coming of the Messiah. Samaritans are outcasts of the Jewish community, and *I* am an outcast of the Samaritan community! I am considered the lowest of the low. Technically, I am "shunned," but I am also treated badly. Mistreated. Assaulted and insulted.

Yes, my wretched life has killed most of my hopes and dreams. I am ostracized and avoided, mostly by the gossiping women who turn their backs and whisper behind their hands. I stay away from temple worship. *God, please be merciful and forgiving.* Even though I don't go to the temple on the Sabbath, I still long for the promised Messiah.

When I go to the marketplace, or to the well for water, I go during the heat of the day to evade the inevitable eyes and comments of disapproval. I am weary! I hardly remember being young and unafraid. I look older than my actual years.

As I walk toward Jacob's Well, I keep my eyes downward—always downward. It is hot and I am tired. Tired of avoiding, tired of pretending, tired of feeling alone. Yet I prefer being alone to being the center of scorn.

Suddenly, I noticed I was not alone at the well. *Oh, no! There is a man, a Jew, at the well! I know He won't speak to me, so I'll just draw the water quickly and leave. I'll pretend I don't see Him. After all, this is our well—not His!*

"May I have a drink of water?"

"What? Why would You ask *me* for a drink? You are a Jew, and You know I am Samaritan." I spoke with some irritation in my voice.

"If you understood God's gifts, and who I am, you would ask *Me* for water. In fact, I offer to you the *Living Water.*"

"Oh, please!" I said sarcastically. "Do You think You are greater than our father Jacob, and all his sons who watered their sheep here? This well is deep, and you have nothing to draw with. Where will you get this 'Living Water?'"

He just smiled. There was something calming and inviting about this Jew sitting on the ground and leaning against the stones of the well. Something far more peaceful and pleasant than other men I knew. I was cautiously drawn to Him. Was it His voice? Was it His behavior toward me? *Me,* the one who was scorned and shunned?

Somehow, I was compelled to help this stranger who looked tired and hot and shading His eyes from the midday sun while looking at me. I lowered my dipper in the jug of water and slowly handed it to Him. "Thank you," He said, then drank it quickly. He seemed to thoroughly enjoy it's coolness.

After I handed Him another dipper-full, He closed His eyes and poured it over His head and beard. We both laughed. What a pleasant laugh!

Again, He told me that He could give *me* water, *living water* that would keep me from ever being thirsty again. I vaguely understood that His *water* was something other than from this well. I wanted this water!

"Go call your husband and return here," He said.

Hmm! Do I tell this Jew I have no husband? No legal husband? I felt obliged to tell the truth. "Sir, I…I don't have a husband."

"Woman, you have spoken honestly! In fact, you have had five husbands, and the man you are living with now is *not* your husband."

Oh no! Is our pleasant exchange going to turn ugly! Is He now going to condemn me? Attack me? Denounce me? So now, being uncomfortable, I wanted to change the subject. "Sir, You must be a prophet. So tell me, our fathers worshiped on this mountain, but you Jews say that true worship is in Jerusalem. There is so much I don't understand. But, in spite of that, when the Messiah comes, I know He will explain it to us. *All* of us!"

"I am He. I am the Messiah!"

I drew in a quick breath and held it for—I don't know how long! Here I was, looking at and talking to the *Messiah!* Could this be true? Yes! No! Yes, I am certain He is the Messiah!

Just then, I saw a bunch of men, more Jews, walking toward the well. Now what? They seemed to know this man and asked why He was talking to me. I backed away from them. Leaving my water jug on the rim of the well, I ran back to town.

Being braver than I thought possible, I told lots of people about the prophet at the well. I said that He knew of my past and was still *kind* to me. Some of the interested townspeople returned to the well with me. They listened to this prophet and invited Him and His friends to stay for a few days in Samaria.

That's when we learned the Jew's name was Jesus, and many came to believe He was the Messiah. The promised Messiah!

Was my life changed? All my life, I had been looking for change in the wrong places. Looking for happiness, security, and love. Now, I found the peace I thought was beyond my grasp—beyond my life. My children have learned about Jesus too. The man I was living with moved out of my house, but he is still helpful to me. It took a while for the women to become accepting, but eventually, a few of them have become my friends. Yes, my life has changed. Changed for the better! I have returned to the temple on Mount Gerizim to worship on the Sabbath.

Nicodemus

Nicodemus (The Pharisee)

My name is Nicodemus. Being a Pharisee and a member of the Sanhedrin, I had a lot of influence among the Jewish people and the religious ruling class. I was a devout orthodox Jew and well-established in our many laws and traditions. I considered myself favored and honored by God. There are many Pharisees, some of them were good men, but many tended to be arrogant and intolerant of the common and lower class of Jews.

Our laws included the Ten Commandments of God, plus the laws of Moses. Many of these statutes were a heavy burden to all Jews and nearly impossible to keep everyone!

Obeying one ordinance seemed to break another. The regulations were either black or white with little or no consideration to kindness or goodwill. We were sticklers for the "letter of the law," but fell desperately short of the "spirit of the law."

To become a Pharisee, and therefore a teacher and upholder of the laws, we were given extensive education regarding the Holy Scriptures. Also, it took a considerable amount of money to buy and secure our positions. We were not only highly regarded because of our religious standing, but for our social status as well.

We looked forward to the coming of the Messiah, This promised Messiah would break the bonds of our oppressors—the hated Romans. He would sit on David's throne and rule forever! Naturally, He would present Himself to our nation as the King. The time was near and we expected Him to arrive as royalty and present Himself triumphantly to *us*—the religious ruling class.

There was an unpretentious evangelist living and preaching on the banks of the Jordan River. His name was John. He attracted lots of people by telling them the Messiah was "at hand," and everyone needed to be ready for His coming. He claimed to be preparing the way for the Son of David. *I don't understand this? Shouldn't the Messiah's announcement be made by someone of a higher social status, not dressed in camel skin and looking rather primitive and wild?* He pleaded for all Jews to repent of their sinful lives and be baptized—the washing away of their old lives, to become new and clean.

Shortly, I heard of an itinerant preacher who was drawing a lot of attention by His preaching and performing miracles! His name was Jesus. Cautiously, and with other Pharisees, I went to see what the attraction was all about. He didn't tell the crowd that He was the Messiah, but spoke as a prophet from God, and told illustrations explaining the kingdom of heaven—as if He *knew!* His speech and gentleness seemed genuinely sincere. His words of rebuke were directed only at us—the Pharisees, priests, lawyers. Strangely, I was drawn to Him! *Why? Only someone from God can talk with such authority and perform these miracles. Yet I have personally seen Him break our Sabbath laws—healing the sick and lame, and telling them to carry their beds. Also, He walks farther on the Sabbath than our laws permit!*

The other Pharisees and lawyers often looked for other ways Jesus was breaking our laws. Once, they saw Him eating without washing His hands and condemned Him for it! I must admit, the "washing" that we do before eating is more of a ritual than actual "cleaning." We dip the tips of our fingers in a bowl and dab them on a towel. Was that considered washing? I seriously doubted it!

Even though I stood among the other Pharisees, I must admit my heart was drawn to Jesus and His word. When I cautiously suggested that Jesus *could* be sent by God, I was strongly reminded that no prophet would ever come from Galilee! I began to search the scriptures foretelling the coming of the Messiah, and found some serious discrepancies from what I read and from what I was taught! I needed to know more!

The history of the Jewish nation was dark by persecuting and killing the prophets of God, resulting in tribulation and even slavery. If Jesus were sent by God, and we followed in the footsteps of our forefathers by not listening to Him, what would be our fate? Disaster? Annihilation?

One night, under the cover of darkness and secrecy, I searched for Jesus. (I wanted to avoid censure and denouncement from the Sanhedrin.) Upon finding Jesus at the Mount of Olives, I felt insecure but tried to appear composed and dignified. "Rabbi, we know that You are a teacher sent by God. You couldn't do the things you do if God was not with You!"

Jesus reply was, "Truly I say, if you want to see the kingdom of heaven, you must be born again."

What? Where did *that* come from? Born again? I wanted to know about *Him*, and He turned it all back to *me!* I remembered that *new* converts were considered "children just born," but I felt no need to change *my* life. I felt secure with God's favor and a place in His kingdom. *How dare Jesus speak to me about not being saved!* So I stammered out a question, "How can a man be born when he is old?" Despite my sarcastic reply, Jesus tenderly and patiently explained to me that being born of the Holy Spirit was necessary for life in the kingdom of heaven. We talked a long time, and I went home feeling blessed and having been in the presence of God.

As time continued, hostility toward Jesus escalated among the priests and Pharisees. He was constantly being questioned with trickery and cunning—hoping to trap Him into saying or doing something they could use against Him. Still, it seemed that the popularity of Jesus increased daily, and throughout all of Judaea. The attention of the people followed Him everywhere, while the influence of the religious ruling class was becoming tenuous. Caiaphas, our High Priest, was losing his control and demanded that Jesus be arrested to "silence Him," stating that the prophet impostor was becoming troublesome and weakening his authority.

In favor of justice, I asked, "Does our law permit us to judge a man without hearing him first?" With a red and contorted face, Caiaphas asked me if I was, also, from Galilee. Reminding me that *no* prophet ever came from Nazareth of Galilee and with a questionable parenthood.

My friend, Joseph of Arimathea, was also a Pharisee. We often talked privately about our growing conviction that Jesus was the Messiah, but we still kept it quiet—just between the two of us. But in the councils, we did what we could to restrain the growing malice, aggression, and hostility toward Jesus. Our bias was not completely unnoticed, however, because we were not invited to other councils concerning Jesus.

Joseph and I were not present at the illegal midnight trial of Jesus. We heard of the false and conflicting accusations flying around the judgment hall. We heard about the betrayer's coins that were thrown *at* Caiaphas, and the scream of terror, "I have sinned and betrayed innocent blood." We heard about the overwhelming contrast in deportment between the red-faced and foul-mouth Caiaphas, and the calm, dignified bearing of Jesus. Yes, we heard about it, but were not present to defend our Lord.

It was later that same day, when I saw Jesus carrying His own cross to be crucified by the Romans—or was He crucified by the religious ruling class of the Jews? Joseph and I stood together at the edge of the crowd. Our hopes and dreams were hanging and dying on that cross. We were ashamed! Ashamed of being associated with the other Pharisees. Ashamed of the cruel cursing and laughing. Ashamed of our weakness in not openly defending and supporting Jesus. We stayed until it was "finished."

Joseph then went to Pilate and asked for the body of Jesus to be buried in his own tomb. The Roman governor didn't believe that Jesus was already dead and sent someone to verify the truth. After that, Joseph, John, and I removed Jesus from the cross. Tenderly and with broken hearts, we washed the bruised and torn flesh of Jesus. Then we wrapped and anointed Him with myrrh and aloes. With deep sorrow and affection, we placed Jesus in Joseph's tomb and rolled the heavy stone in front of the entrance.

This act of touching a dead body—even the body of Jesus—now denied us the right to participate in the Passover services. Yet we could do no other. No greater honor!

What I was reluctant to do while Jesus was alive, I now became bold in proclaiming Him to be the Messiah. After Jesus returned to His Father in heaven, my influence and money helped the followers of Jesus set up their new church. I gave to all I had to help proclaim the good news of salvation through Jesus Christ our Lord.

Woman

The Woman (The Accused)

I was married to a good man, kind and gentle. He gave me riches and a nice home, but I didn't love him. I sought the company of other men who gave me many more gifts of jewelry, fine clothes, and wine. Sometimes, I would be gone for several days, but my husband always came looking for me, declaring his love and pleading for me to return. We had several children, which is to say, *I* had several children and by different men. My husband loved and raised them as his own. *Why? Why can't I be the kind of wife and mother I should be?*

Our home was several miles from Jerusalem, but I wanted and needed the excitement of the larger city—and the richer men. At first, I tried to stay clear of the Pharisees and other religious leaders, until some of them started paying *special* attention to me. This was especially exciting since it was *forbidden!* I knew it was wrong. I knew it was sin! Still…

Being Jewish, I was familiar with the Commandments of God, which were given to Moses on Mt. Sinai. At first, my adulterous actions bothered my conscience, but as time and men continued, my moral ethics became vague. The line between right and wrong grew faint and obscured. Still, to avoid public exposure and censure, I knew enough to conceal my actions to secret chambers in the sweet hours of darkness.

I also knew that Moses' law permitted a man to divorce his wife if she was unfaithful. Why didn't my husband divorce me? Why did he always come looking for me and forgive my infidelity? Somehow the historical account in Holy Scripture of Hosea and Gomer nagged at my heart—our stories were vastly similar.

Early one morning, just as the stars began to fade and the streets were still quiet, several men crashed through the door of my overnight room, the room I was sharing with a man I had met last evening. The clamor suddenly awakened me and the stranger lying beside my naked body. The men were all shouting and accusing me of infidelity and adultery. *Yes, but it takes two to commit adultery, and my bed partner is not being accused? No one is shouting vile words at him! No one is pointing their gnarly fingers at him! Is he in on this? Besides all this, I recognize two of the Pharisees as having been with me a few nights ago. How dare they!*

The seething group began pulling at me. They reminded me that Moses' law said that adulterers should be stoned to death. They didn't give me time to get dressed, so I just grabbed a small blanket off the bed to wrap around my naked body.

Dogs were barking as the men were running and dragging me in my bare feet through the streets of Jerusalem. With stones in their hands, it seemed like they were looking for something, or someone. After a while, as the early morning eastern sun shone brightly on the temple walls, one of them shouted, "There He is!"

They shoved me in front of a man standing quietly and alone. This seemed strange to me as He was not dressed in the elaborate and expensive clothes of the religious rulers—my accusers. Why did they drag me through the streets looking for Him? He appeared to have no authority over my situation. I stood before Him trying to cover my shivering body. Shivering from the cold, the shame, and fear. In my humiliation, I could not look directly at His face, but neither did I feel threatened by Him. Again, the accusations of adultery filled the morning air. "We caught this woman in the very act of adultery. Moses' law commands us that such sinners should be stoned. What do You say?"

It was quiet now, waiting for His answer. Then after looking around at the Pharisees and other religious rulers holding large stones in their white-knuckled hands, He knelt down and began writing in the dust of the street. The merciless crowd drew closer to see what He was writing.

After a few moments, the man stood up and said to the plotting accusers, "You are correct. So let those of you who are sinless cast the first stone at this woman." I knew those men, and they were just as guilty as I, but I still dreaded and feared the first stone hitting my trembling body.

Now with my head down and my eyes closed, I heard the thud of a stone falling to the street. Then I heard several more stones being dropped. I cautiously looked around and saw the men walking away! All the men and their stones were gone!

The man now standing before me, asked, “Woman, where are your accusers? Isn’t anyone left to condemn you?”

“No, sir. They are all gone!”

“Neither do I condemn you. Go now and sin no more!”

I discovered the man’s name was Jesus. The man who saved me from my death sentence and my sins. Yes, my life has changed! I went back to my forgiving husband and my children, a changed and thankful woman. Now when I occasionally leave my home and family, I spend it following Jesus and assisting wherever I can in serving Him.

Herod Antipas (The King of the Jews)

My father, Herod the Great, was awarded the title King of the Jews in Judaea by the Roman Senate. He ruled from year 37 to 4 BC. He had ten wives and fourteen sons along with daughters. I was educated, along with my brothers, in Rome.

I lived in fear for my life, and the life of my mother, Multhace. There was a lot of political strife and scheming. I was surrounded by murder of family members, executions, lying, plotting, drunkenness, adultery, and incest. My father exhibited debilitating depression, paranoia, and fits of rage.

One year toward the end of his reign, a group of magi from the East came to his palace in Jerusalem. It was an impressive entourage of wealth and influence that caused a commotion among the people. They asked to have an audience with the king regarding the mysterious star they had followed to the capital city.

My father, an Edomite and loosely of Jewish descent, was vaguely acquainted with the prophecies of the Jews. Being very paranoid, along with wild threats, he called the priests and scribes to search the scriptures that he may be well versed before talking to the magi. The priests told my father that it was foretold of a ruler who would be born in Bethlehem.

To calm his rage and tantrum, he quickly drank some strong wine. When the magi were finally given audience, Herod the Great looked composed and tranquil. Through an interpreter, the magi told of their interest in the star and the new king. They wished to honor this king with appropriate gifts.

Feigning joy and interest toward this usurper to his throne, he asked that the magi go to Bethlehem then bring back word of His location that he may also pay homage. But when the magi didn't return, my father was livid! Outrage turned to violence. Violence with a *plan!*

The plan was to prevent anyone from taking the kingdom from him—Herod the Great! He would have every boy child, two years old and under *killed!* Bethlehem was a small town and probably no more than twenty babies were killed, but it was still an extremely cruel strategy.

Not long after that, Herod the Great succumbed to an illness that the doctors could not cure. He suffered long with great pain, which of course, added to his rage and paranoia. He knew there would not be any mourning at his death, so he ordered the executions of influential men to be carried out when he died. This order was not supported nor done. True to his paranoid prediction, there was no mourning, but rejoicing upon his death.

Now Rome divided Herod the Great's empire between three of his sons. My half-brother, Archelaus was given one-half. My brother, Phillip, was given one-fourth. And I, Antipas, was given one-fourth.

Enough—enough of *history!* Now, let's get to *my* story! I was married first to Phasaelis. It was a political and arranged marriage, and she was rather dull and unattractive. We had nothing in common, which didn't matter. She could be formally attired and elegantly adorned to sit on her throne beside me at diplomatic or social functions.

At one of the courts festivities, with lots of food, wine, and dancing, I noticed my brother's ex-wife, Herodias, looking especially attractive. Seductive and alluring!

We caught each other's eye, and I motioned for her to join me. "Come, sit on a cushion close to my throne." She was heavily painted, bejeweled, and sparsely dressed. She moved with flirtatious gestures. Very appealing!

I wanted her for my wife, but what should I do with Phasaelis? Why was there such an uproar over my wanting to marry Herodias? After all, my father had ten wives and unknown adulterous and incestuous affairs. "So if I want Herodias, I will *have her!*"

My divorce from Phasaelis and marriage to Herodias happened so close together I was never sure which came first. Plus, there was so much intermarrying and incest, I couldn't be sure that Herodias wasn't somehow related to me. She and her daughter, Salome, moved into my castle.

Shortly after my marriage to Herodias, an irritating itinerate preacher began accusing me of adultery and incest. As annoying as it was, I wasn't nearly as infuriated as my wife. She kept asking and *nagging* me to "do something" about this man called John the Baptist.

Finally, I acquiesced. I had John arrested and thrown in prison. That, of course, didn't stop him! He continued to accuse and tell everyone he saw of my sins. It was becoming a friction between Herodias and myself.

To demonstrate my unconcerned attitude toward John's allegations, I threw a grand birthday party for myself. Lots of food, wine, music, and dancing! It started early in the day and lasted late that night and into the next day.

Seeing my stepdaughter, Salome, swaying seductively to the music, I called to her to dance for us—*for me!* She refused. *She can't refuse me!* But in my drunken state, I was having too much pleasure to threaten. So I made a promise to her, in front of my guests, that she could have *anything* she wanted—up to half of my kingdom. Salome's well-groomed eyebrows shot up and her alluring red lips smiled. She walked sensually to her mother. They whispered for a while; then she returned, prepared to please my guests, and *me!* What a dance! Sultry! Provocative!

After it was over, Salome landed at my feet. She was breathing hard and moist with perspiration. She looked into my dilated eyes, and I again promised to give her anything she wanted. Between rapid respirations, she announced, "I want the *head* of John the Baptist on a silver platter and brought to this party."

I looked around the banquet hall at the faces of my drunken guests, who were now quiet and looking at me for my reaction. I was horrified and looked for someone, *anyone,* to object—to give me strength. How could I do this? Yes, I had ordered lots of executions by beheadings, and John was definitely a thorn in my flesh, but somehow, I rather liked him. Or was I just afraid of him? We'd had several private conversations, and there was something about John that interested and intrigued me, and I secretly believed that he was a prophet. A man of God! I did not want to behead him but was held to my drunken promise or lose face. Protocol demanded I keep my word. The word of a *king!*

"You *promised!*" she said. "You said I could have *anything* I wanted. Well?"

"Yes, my sweet, I *did* promise." Salome's beauty was now repulsive to me. Her charm and appeal turned sour! Sour wine! After looking into the eyes of this vixen for several moments and glancing over at the smiling lips of Herodias, I nodded and waved my hand at the guards. Order given!

The bloodied head of John the Baptist was brought to the banquet hall amid a few cheers, and many groans. Needless to say, the party ended. No more music! No dancing! Just mumbling while my guests left. Left me to my thoughts. My regrets! My weakness!

Accusations from the Baptist were now silenced! But the accusations echoed! Echoed in the streets, in the palace, and in my bedchamber. The echoes were loudest at night, keeping me awake and tossing endlessly. No rest! No peace! My wife, however, expressed sheer delight over her *victory*, but forbade me to ever see Salome again. After a few months, I was finally able to put the whole contemptible mess out of my mind.

Sometime later, during one of the Jewish Passovers, Pilate, the Governor of Judea, sent a troublesome prisoner to me for judgment. He came with a large entourage of soldiers, Jewish dignitaries, and curiosity-seekers. I had heard of this man as one who was performing miracles in Judea, and I longed to see if He were John the Baptist raised to life. This man was accused of being a traitor, a blasphemer, and doing His miracles through the power of Beelzebub—the devil. I had seen and judged many men who were rightly accused. But the accusations toward this dignified and composed man appeared distorted. The charges were obviously made through malice and envy.

I questioned Jesus at length, and offered Him freedom if He would perform some miracle for me and the assembly. "Just one miracle," I said, "Just one, and I will dismiss these charges against You." The prisoner gave no evidence that He even heard me. *The nerve of Him!* I could have tolerated an argument or even a reproof. Reprove my life of sin and murder. But His silence seemed to me the severest rebuke. He seemed indifferent to my authority. His silence irritated me! He ignored my threats. He ignored *me!* Months ago, I had ignored the words and the pleadings from the Baptist, and now I, the *king*, was being ignored!

Infuriated, I accused this prisoner of being a fake—an impostor. I told the mob they could do what they wanted with Him. If my soldiers had not stepped in, the mob would have killed Him in my presence. Because I was unwilling to pass a guilty verdict on Jesus, and yet unwilling to set Him free, I joined the mob in ridiculing and humiliating Him. After having Jesus flogged, I placed a purple robe over His bleeding shoulders and returned Him to Pilate.

Later, I heard that Jesus was crucified, not by the *orders* of Pilate, but by his weakness. I guess Pilate and I have more in common than I realized.

Has my life changed after meeting Jesus? You tell me! The year is now 39 AD; my wife, Herodius, and I have been exiled to Gall. I don't know where Salome is. All of my wealth, my possessions, and my position as King of the Jews have been given to Herod Agrippa by Caligula, the Emperor of Rome. My coldness, my hardness, and my sinful life became more evident to me and those around me after the beheading of John the Baptist. Seeing Jesus and doing nothing to save or justify Him, was my final crime of weakness that led to my ruin and humiliation. The last hammer nail!

Pilate

Pontius Pilate (The Governor of Judaea)

Promoted? I was ordered by Tiberius Caesar to replace Valerius Gratus in Judaea as prefect/governor in 26 AD. This looked like a military promotion, but in Judaea? Fleas and scorpions! The area is hot and sultry, both atmospherically and politically. A steaming bed of rebellion! Yet here was a good possibility of riches through taxes.

My home was in Caeserea, but I needed to reside occasionally in Jerusalem during the Jewish high religious holidays, and especially during their Passover week. That is a time when hundreds of thousands of pilgrims from all over the world come to celebrate their traditional liberation from Egypt of many years ago. And now they continually talk about their liberation from Rome, "Poor buggers, that's not likely!"

Since the Jewish leaders forbid the Roman denarius to be used in their temple, the pilgrims have to exchange their money into shekels to pay their temple tax. There is, of course, an exorbitant fee for this exchange. A tax to pay a tax! If the pilgrims cannot afford the temple tax, the priests "loaned" them the money at unreasonably high interest rates. Many have lost their homes, their property, or their freedom for inability to repay the "loans." The rich, religious, ruling class get richer!

So here I came with my wife, Claudia. She was not happy about this move, but felt, as I did, this could be a good political move. I just needed to keep Herod Antipas, and especially Tiberius Caesar, happy. A narrow and slippery slope! I had been given a garrison of three thousand soldiers to utilize in keeping law and order.

While Gratus was governor, he appointed Joseph Caiaphas as High Priest. Having the position of High Priest is an extremely important and powerful status in the Jewish religion. I needed to ally myself with Caiaphas in order to attempt harmony between Romans and Jews. It was obvious that he had immense wealth and carried himself with a superior and aloof manner. He was cold and calculating and openly expressed resentment toward Rome, even though his position and wealth are in cooperation and conjunction with Rome! *I don't trust him!* All the same, we feigned friendship for the good of quid pro quo.

For about ten years, I maintained law and order in Judea, trying to keep the Jews under Roman control, and Tiberius satisfied. Control! Judgments! Tax collections! Executions!

This year, Claudia and I again traveled back to Jerusalem for another Passover, which was showing signs of being especially unruly. It was reported to me that at the beginning of Passover week, thousands of Jews were waving palm branches and yelling "King, King. King of the Jews." Also, someone upset the money tables in the Gentiles' courtyard of the temple and set all the animals free. I am so tired of all this. All this unrest. All this rebellion. This strange religion with animal sacrifice. This *one* God. These strict and meticulous rules. *Yes, I need to be here to maintain some semblance of order.*

Very early on the Friday of Jewish Passover week, I was awakened and expected to settle yet another dispute. *Aaaaagh! Will this week never end?*

I reluctantly got out of bed and agreed to meet with the complainants at the usual judgment hall. But, since this was their Holy Week, they could not "defile" themselves by coming into the hall. They requested the judgment be made in the courtyard. *This must be pretty important at this time of morning, and on this day of Passover week! This poor bugger must be a real problem and threat to them!* Apparently, they had already tried this man, and wanted my stamp of approval. *I don't care! Just one less troublemaker.* Approve. Stamp. Done. Easy enough!

The elaborately dressed fat cats of the Jewish ruling class were all yelling at once. They were demanding an execution of one of their own. They can have a trial and punish an offender, but cannot legally kill someone. Only Rome can execute a man. I have heard that occasionally they will "stone" someone to death. But that is hard to prove and bring to trial.

It was hard to understand their vehement behavior toward what appeared to be a calm and dignified man. I had sentenced many hardened criminals, and *probably* some who were not worthy of death. Guilty or innocent—no matter. But nothing I saw or heard from these Jewish religious leaders seemed worthy of this man's death. Here standing before me was *dignity, calmness, nobility*. Looking directly into the eyes of this man, I was strangely unnerved and shaken. I felt weak and impotent. I cleared my throat, squared my shoulders, and tried my best to sound indifferent. "What accusation do you bring against this man?"

There were conflicting allegations, and finally *I* was accused of trivializing the power and important status of Caiaphas and the Sanhedrin. It was demanded that I take their *word* for His guilt and punishment, but I could see through their accusations. I didn't for a minute believe them. *Something else is going on here. I hate these Jews!*

Finally, someone yelled that He was in rebellion against Rome. *Yeah, so what else is new?* He was accused of not paying His taxes and calling himself a king. I had heard stories of this Jesus and wanted to learn more about Him, but the mob was so loud and unruly. I pulled the prisoner aside and asked if He was *really* a king. Admitting He was a king, but not of this world, didn't help my cause any. On the other hand, setting Himself up as a king could be considered treason, and that would be Herod's problem, who just happens to be in Jerusalem now. Good! No longer *my* problem! Shift the responsibility! "Take the accused to Herod!"

With that decision, a riot broke out and it looked like they were going to kill this man right here and now—right in front of me! Threats and accusations were flying everywhere, even toward me. Threats like, "You are no friend of Rome. You can be sure, Caesar will hear of this!"

Two or three hours later, the mob headed by the Jewish leaders brought their hated prisoner back. He was dressed in a dirty royal robe. It was most irritating to me having them back in my courtyard. He had been severely beaten. And seeing Him wearing that royal robe sent chills down my back! Impatiently, I asked, "What do you want me to do? I have questioned this man and find no fault in Him. Therefore, I will have Him beaten *again* and released." I realized that was cowardly of me, but perhaps that would soften their hatred. Flogging this innocent man just to pacify a mob was barbaric and inhumane. Appease! Compromise!

Once again, this Jew was standing in front of me, now weak, bleeding heavily, and wearing a crown! Someone had made a crown of thorns, and pushed the thorns deep into His flesh. I felt sick to my stomach.

How can I satisfy my conviction of His innocence and comply with the bloodthirsty mob? I knew what I should do, but having crossed and obscured the line of justice so many times in the past, it was hard to know exactly where that line was anymore.

Unexpectedly, a soldier thrust a note into my hand. Looking around, I saw my wife, Claudia, standing in the shadows. Reading the note made me feel faint, nauseated, and confused. She wrote, "Have nothing to do with this righteous man. I have had troubled sleep because of Him." I got a premonition like I had never experienced before! I broke out in a cold sweat and seemed to foresee my own future.

Because of the heightened yelling, I needed to act. Act quickly! Suddenly, I thought of a clever plan. I remembered an ancient custom of the Jews to release a prisoner at Passover. Quickly, I gave orders to some soldiers to bring out Barabbas who was condemned to be crucified soon with two other criminals. Surely, having Jesus and Barabbas standing side by side would convince them of their fallacy. They feared Barabbas, as did *everyone!*

Barabbas was brought out in strong chains by four soldiers. He was foul-mouthed! Threatening! Spitting! A striking contrast between the two men. Raising my arms, I *tried* for several minutes to quiet the rioting mob. The noise remained almost deafening. At that point, I motioned the soldiers forward to show the united power of Rome. *It seems they have more fear of the soldiers than they do of me!* After I got their attention, I offered them the choice of a prisoner-release. "Barabbas or Jesus?" Someone shouted, "Barabbas." Then growing in volume, they yelled, "Give us Barabbas, give us Barabbas." Over and over, they yelled for Barabbas. Amazing! Truly perplexing!

At first, I thought they misunderstood their choice of prisoner to be *released!* No, they understood perfectly. Their thirst for the blood of Jesus would not be appeased.

"What then shall I do with this Jesus?"

"Crucify Him! Crucify Him! Crucify Him!"

"Shall I crucify your king?"

"Yes, crucify Him! We have no king but Caesar!"

That was it! I had revealed my weakness. My vacillating character. My fear of coercion. There was no backing down now, and the horde will have their way. Still, I didn't want to take the blame. I asked the suffering prisoner before me, "Where do you come from?" But when He didn't answer me, I added, "Don't You understand? I have the power to release You, or to crucify You?"

His response was, "You have no power over Me except what has been given to you from above." *Above? I knew He wasn't talking about Rome!* "And the ones that delivered Me to you have the greater blame."

I then requested a basin of water to be brought to me. And before the briefly quieted throng, I ceremoniously washed my hands, dried them on a towel, and angrily threw it at the demon-possessed mob.

After that, I walked over to Jesus and put my hand on His bleeding but regal shoulder. Turning to the frenzied multitude, I said, "Behold the man. I find no fault in Him. Do whatever you want with Him, and may His blood be on you!" At that announcement, the soldiers took Jesus and two other criminals to be crucified. Barabbas was free!

The courtyard was trashed! It would take some time to clean up the broken vessels, stones, tree branches. Such swine!

Now sitting alone, and not wanting to face Claudia, I scribbled out a sign to be hung on the cross, above the head of Jesus. "Jesus of Nazareth, King of the Jews."

Shortly, an angry delegation came to *complain* about the sign I had written. *Really?* "Can't you be satisfied you have crucified a just and righteous Man? An innocent man? A God? What I have written, I have written! Now, get out!"

Has my life changed since the trial and crucifixion of Jesus? It was many weeks, perhaps months, before I could get a decent night's sleep. Terrible nightmares and stomach cramps. My wife, Claudia, left me. Rumors are that she has joined the "Christians."

I walked a narrow and slippery path between keeping order in Judaea and being reported to Rome for my increasingly cruel actions. Vitellius, the Roman governor of Syria, sent me to Rome to explain to Tiberius my actions during the massacre of the Samaritans. However, before I had my trial, Tiberius died, and the powerful and cruel Caligula took the Roman seat. Not a good omen for me.

Mary

Mary (The Mother)

No mother could be prouder of a son than I was of mine! I held all the precious moments foretelling of His birth deep in my heart—the shepherds in the stable, the old man and woman in the temple at His dedication, the wise men of the East, and hundreds of other indications of His holy life and purpose. Yes, many times my heart ached for my Son, and my tears welled at seeing the hostility and rejection of those especially close to Him.

One frightening event happened on our trip to Jerusalem for Passover. Jesus was only twelve, but seemed intensely interested in the Passover events. He knew the story well about the Israelite slaves fleeing Egypt and their crossing the Red Sea by the grace and power of God. While other children of His age took little interest in the Passover events, Jesus seemed to understand a *deeper* meaning—deeper than even I understood.

After Passover and all our things had been gathered up, we left with our friends and families. We assumed Jesus was with the other children of His age, but when we stopped for the night, He wasn't among our traveling group! He was nowhere to be found. How could Joseph and I be so careless? After His birth, we had to flee to Egypt to protect Him from being killed by Herod. We still needed to protect this Child of God, but we lost sight of Him and failed. Failed miserably!

Returning to Jerusalem, it took us three days to find our precious Son. We found Him sitting among the rabbis and learned men and discussing with them the sacred scriptures and prophecy. Running to Him, I reprimanded, saying, "Why didn't You stay with our group? We have been worried and looking for You. Why have You treated us like this?"

In His gentle way, He replied, "Mother, don't you know that I must be about My Father's business?" *His father? Joseph is His father!* Then I remembered the words of the angel and how this Holy Child was conceived. *Does Jesus really understand His life, His mission, the prophecy of His sitting on David's throne?*

Jesus grew and was always helpful. Being so tenderhearted, He occasionally found some wounded animal that He brought home as a pet until it was well enough to go back into the wild. It always saddened Him to see the other children being cruel to some animal or to each other.

He worked hard beside His father, Joseph, in the carpenter shop. His craftsmanship was unparalleled and He could design something very beautiful out of an old piece of wood. Turning it over and over in His creative hands, He could imagine and make something beautiful and useful. After Joseph died, Jesus stayed working to support our simple home. I realized that His time in the shop would eventually end. With the words still ringing in my head, "I must be about my *Father's* business," I realized His time here was coming to a close.

Then one day, with the sawdust and wood shavings brushed off His clothes, He came into the house. He gave me an endearing and precious smile, then a very long and tender hug. He whispered only, "My Father's business." Slowly, He turned and walked out the door. I watched the puffs of dust from His sandals as He walked down the dirt road. With tears running down my cheeks, I wanted to call Him back. Back home! Back to me! But, I knew He must go and be about His "Father's business."

A few months later, while at a wedding feast of the bridal party related to us, Jesus came with some of His friends. He had lost a lot of weight, and I was concerned for Him. Still, He had an aura of purity, peace, and dignity. I longed for Jesus to demonstrate to the people at this feast, His heavenly mission and being the honored of God.

Because I was a relative of the couple, I did what I could to help with the serving and the catering of their many guests. Toward the end of the celebration, there was still plenty of food, but the wine was gone! This would be a terrible embarrassment to the host as it would show poor planning and hospitality. *Can Jesus help? Will He?* After telling Jesus of the wine dilemma, He gave me a tender kiss and said, "Mother, what does that have to do with Me? The hour of My work has not come."

Still, I told those at the serving table, "Do whatever my Son tells you to do!"

Six large stone jars were empty and Jesus told the servants to fill them with water.

"Water? Just water? Is this a joke?" they said to each other. But something in His manner compelled them to do as they were told. And upon their first dip and taste, they were astonished and took some to the host who was unaware of the shortage. He immediately took some to the bridegroom and asked him why the best wine was saved for last. This miracle of turning water into the best wine spread throughout the region, even as far as Jerusalem. I was so proud of my Son.

Over the next three years, I occasionally traveled with the women, who, along with His disciples, followed Jesus. His miracles were wonderful, His preaching was inspiring to all—even the children! Wherever He went, crowds pressed close to Him. He spoke with unparalleled authority, and His popularity grew daily. *Oh, how I wish He would proclaim Himself King and sit on David's throne now, and break the iron chains of Rome.* Strange to me, however, was His talk of betrayal and death and that His kingdom was not of this world. Where did He get those ideas? Certainly not from *me!*

Two special events occurred at the beginning of Passover. The first was when Jesus rode on a young donkey into the city of Jerusalem. It was thrilling to see and hear how the people were waving palm branches and shouting, "Hail to the King! Hosanna! Hosanna to the Son of David!" The second event was when Jesus arrived at the temple courtyard, and drove out the money changers and overturned their tables. He set free the birds and sheep. (He had done this one other time.) *I understand there is corruption by the temple money changers, but I wish Jesus would not antagonize the priests and Pharisees. They can help Him. Or they can ruin Him!*

On Friday morning, one of Jesus' disciples, John, came to my door. "Come quickly! Jesus has been tried by both Herod and Pilate and condemned to be executed—crucified! I will take you there and will stay with you. Come!"

"What? That can't be!" It is a terrible thing to hear that one's son is to be executed, even if he were a scoundrel. But *my* Son is pure, sinless, ordained by God! His holy mission is to save Israel and break the bonds of Rome!

"Yes, John! Please take me to Him, quickly! Is there anything we can do?" *How can I challenge Rome? How can I plead for the life of my Son, a sinless Man? Surely Yahweh, our Heavenly Father, will not allow this to happen! Surely!*

The crowds were thick and unruly. Pushing! Shoving! Yelling! Where was the multitude of several days ago that sang, "Hosanna to the King of Kings?" Where were those who were healed, raised from the dead, ate the bread, and proclaimed Him to be the Messiah? Where were His disciples, His supporters? Where was that glorious and powerful angel who warned Joseph and me to hide Him from Herod?

When John and I got to Golgotha, I heard iron hitting iron. It was the nailing of my precious Son, my innocent Child to that hideous implement of torture and slow death. Again the words predicting that *my* heart would be pierced came to mind. *Yes, my heart is pierced! My heart is breaking! Unspeakable grief! No mother should ever witness this!* I wanted to run! I wanted to stay! I wanted to scream and yell! Yes, even yell at God! My Son was going to *die*, and all the hopes and dreams for Israel's future were broken. Our Roman bonds were stronger than ever! Israel's Savior was now hanging on a cross and *dying! Can I—can* we *have been so wrong?*

Besides Jesus' physical pain, there must have been tremendous emotional agony for Him to see me so distraught and broken. But I couldn't help it! There was nothing I could do to relieve His misery and suffering. Finally, looking at me and nodding toward John, He said, "Mother, *there* is your son." Then looking at John, "There is your mother." I nearly fainted, but John held me up. He supported me in his strong arms, and we walked together off that cruel death rock. The rock that dashed Israel's hope.

John took me to his house and stayed with me until he said, "Mary, I hate to leave you now, but I must see if I can find the others. *All* of us ran and abandoned Him when He needed us most. I am so sorry and ashamed! When I find them, I will come for you."

Has my life changed having known Jesus? It began to change over thirty years ago when Jesus was just a baby, and I was a very young woman. He was my God-given Son to raise for the Heavenly Kingdom, even though I didn't fully understand His mission until after His death and resurrection. His ascension to heaven was both sad and exhilarating. And I will one day see Him on His heavenly throne and sitting beside His Father.

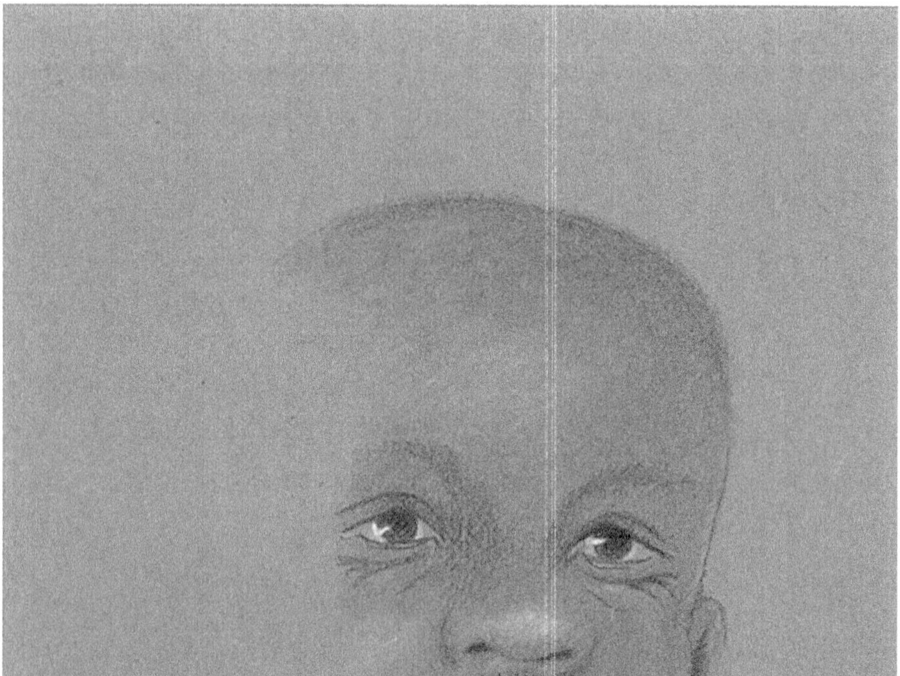
Simon

Simon (From Cyrene)

My home was originally in Cyrene, a town with many Jews in Northern Africa by the sea. My sons, Alexander and Rufus, and I came to Judaea to work. We are strangers in this land and live in the countryside as itinerant farmers. We generally try to avoid the towns, but occasionally have to go there to buy supplies.

Jerusalem in Judaea seems to be a hot bed of rebellion and on the verge of revolt. It is not uncommon to see fights and small riots. Rome rules here, or at least tries to. The governors and soldiers are harsh and cruel to those in resistance. One time, I heard that a Jew overturned all the money tables in their temple. Apparently everyone was afraid and ran from Him. But since it happened in the temple courtyard, the soldiers did nothing. I also heard they kind of enjoyed watching the money changers and Pharisees on the run.

My sons told me about a preacher who was making a huge impact on the people. He did miracles of healing the sick or crippled. He talked of a new Kingdom, of a new life, a new creation. There was talk about Him being the Messiah, the Christ. He was even hailed "King of the Jews." *Hmmm...He better be careful!*

One Friday, during the Jewish Passover week, I went into Jerusalem. I heard taunting and mocking, "Make way for the King of the Jews." Curiosity led me to the commotion. It was a disgusting spectacle of hate, which included their religious leaders and the riffraff from the streets.

The center of attention, the "King of the Jews," had been arrested and condemned to die by Rome. Of course, that meant crucifixion. This poor man had been severely beaten and appeared extremely weak. Too weak to carry His own means of death on His shoulders. Falling under the heavy cross, the soldiers yelled, threatened, whipped, and kicked Him. *No matter what this man has done, He doesn't deserve this treatment. My heart goes out to Him. I pity Him!*

Suddenly, a strong hand grabbed my arm. I jerked my head around and looked directly into the face of a fierce Roman soldier. He forced me to lift the cross off the condemned man's back and carry it for Him. After I hoisted the cross, I offered my free arm to the man and helped Him to His feet. This man, who was suffering extreme pain and humiliation, whispered, "Thank you."

"Thank you?" In His suffering, He said, "Thank you." I hadn't volunteered for this! I was *forced!* Forced by a Roman soldier with a spear! Maybe the soldier saw some compassion in my eyes for this man. On the other hand, seeing this totally exhausted man, I might have offered my help anyway. I like to think I would!

We trudged slowly up the hill to the site of Roman torture and executions. I had seen these implements of death at a distance. But never up close, and certainly never involved with its purpose!

Upon arrival, I wanted to leave. Leave this horrible scene, this commotion, this performance. But I couldn't. Just couldn't! *What is the matter with me? Why am I drawn to this place? Why am I drawn to this man? I don't like being in the company of these undignified and shameful brutes shouting insults at a dying man!* They made fun of Him and chided, "If you really are the Messiah, the Son of God, come down and we will believe You." I wanted to help Him more, but it was too late.

There was a vast variety of extreme emotions surrounding the cross. Some of the onlookers were crying, some were laughing, some were hurling insults and threats. All of them seemed to have a personal interest in the suffering man in the center. And all of nature seemed to respond to this turmoil. There was a strange and eerie darkness at midday. There was thunder and lightning. Lightning hitting trees and buildings. Lightning that seemed to come *from* the cross. There was an occasional bright light that broke through the clouds and shone on the center cross. *Who is this man? Can He really be the Jewish Messiah, the King of the Jews?*

After this Jesus of Nazareth (as was written on the sign above His head), cried out in a strong voice, "It is finished." A few moments later, he died. It was over for Him! No more pain. No more suffering. No more humiliation. Again, the earth seemed to rebel. It rebelled with a violent earthquake that destroyed buildings and rearranged rocks and mountains! *Who was this Man? Could He really be the Jewish Messiah, the King of the Jews?*

I walked slowly away from this place. I had much to think about and much to consider, but first, I must look for my sons. They had to hear about this!

Was my life changed? How could it not? After hearing about the resurrection of the man Jesus, my life took on a whole new meaning. Several days later, while I was in Jerusalem, I met Jesus face to face. He looked lovingly in my eyes and again whispered, "Thank you." Tears, uncontrollable tears, rolled down my face. I wanted to give my life in service to this beautiful Savior, this Man who was indeed the Messiah, the King of the Jews, the Son of God.

Thief

The Thief (On the Cross)

Being Jewish, I was, of course, taught to hate Rome and the Romans and to look forward to the promised Messiah who would break our oppression. My hate was stronger than my hope, and my life took me into rebellion. I seemed to always be looking for…I don't know…something. Excitement! Revolution!

Living on the edge, my life took on one offense or misdemeanor after another. I ran with a group of wild and dangerous ruffians. In and out of prison for stealing and occasional violence to young and old. Rome's favorite execution for Jews is crucifixion—a slow and a most ignominious way to die. I had witnessed many. Still, that did not dissuade my savage and wild choices.

My last trial was truly my last. I was finally sentenced and scheduled to be executed for a major crime against society with two other human failures! No way out. I had reached the point of no return. As much as I hated this last verdict, I had to admit it was justified punishment. I hated myself. I hated everyone. I had nothing more to live for!

While waiting in the dark and filthy cells for our sentences to be carried out, we heard the shouting of a mob coming from Pilate's courtyard. An extremely chilling noise. We did not understand its meaning but assumed it was probably another trial of a truly dangerous and corrupt criminal. He would, no doubt, be joining us. Joining the death parade to the rock.

After a while, we heard the clanging of the jailer's keys, and four Roman soldiers came to the cell that held Barabbas—the man with the most dangerous and violent reputation! They chained and removed him. Josh and I looked at each other and wondered if we were next. Shortly, we heard the name, "Barabbas," " Barabbas," and "Crucify him!" "Crucify him!" *We know our sentences are the Roman cross, so why are they now yelling for him to be crucified? Even though I know my execution is near, it is still bone-chilling to hear a mob screaming for my death.*

Later, soldiers came for Josh and me. We were told that Barabbas was set free in exchange for a man accused of insurrection and treason against Rome. Upon arriving to the courtyard in my own chains, I was shocked to see the "criminal" who was exchanged for Barabbas. It was obvious He had been severely flogged with strips of His flesh hanging from His back and chest, and standing in His own pool of blood.

There was something about this man that was strangely familiar. He was calm and poised despite His severe and obvious pain. He had a kingly bearing and was wearing a crown of *thorns*!

My thoughts were abruptly ended when we were roughly pushed outside the courtyard. Our crosses were cruelly shoved upon our backs. Josh and I were still strong enough and filled with enough hate that we carried our crosses with bold defiance. Hate! Defiance!

All the way through the city, I followed a blood path. Blood from the poor wretch ahead of me! There was yelling and jeering from the bloodthirsty mob. Some of the women were crying and showing sympathy, but no one offered to help this friendless and beaten man. All attention seemed to be on this "treasonous" criminal, they were totally ignoring Josh and me.

Our death procession stopped briefly when the man fell again under His heavy load. The drunken soldiers whipped and kicked Him. Finally, a large and strong-looking man was roughly yanked from the crowd and told to carry His cross. After taking the burden on his own shoulders, he offered a helping arm to the exhausted prisoner. In a dry whisper, I heard the man say, "Thank you."

Again—where had I seen this man they called "Jesus"? Those two words, "Thank you," rang a vague memory. Yes! I heard this man, Jesus, talking to a multitude on a hillside. Rich and thrilling were His words of a heavenly kingdom. His words were comforting, and I was convicted of my life of crime and wanted to know more. Yet, I was confused.

So I went to one of the rabbis for clarification. He said, "Jesus was just another man claiming to be sent from God. The Pharisees and lawyers will *know* when the Messiah is here among us. They are God's instruments for the Jews, not this common rabble from Nazareth who (by the way) breaks the Sabbath." Adding, "The Pharisees are given power by God to uphold and interpret His laws and denounce those who break them."

As I left the rabbi, I thought, *There are so many, many laws, who can keep them—or, keep from breaking them? I wonder!* Strange, how this rabbi didn't denounce me for my life of sin! So I gave up my conviction to learn more about this Jesus and returned with stronger resolve to rebel. I plunged deeper and deeper into sin and hate. Hate for Rome, hate for Jewish laws and traditions, and hate for myself. Being a Jew, I knew what sin was, but I didn't care!

Upon arrival to the dreaded and infamous crucifixion site, the soldiers tied us to the crosses with strong ropes before driving the spikes into our flesh. Josh and I resisted, fought, screamed, and swore. We swore at the Roman guards, the curious onlookers, the elaborately-dressed priests and Pharisees, and the vindictive mob—all yelling at once. The only quiet person was Jesus. He put up no resistance! His only sounds were justified groans and a quiet prayer of forgiveness for His persecutors. Amazing!

The courtly and rich clothing worn by the Pharisees, priests, and other religious rulers seemed incongruous to their foul language and obscene gestures—all directed at Jesus. Language and gestures I had heard and seen only in prison cells! They laughed and said to Jesus, the suffering man in the middle, "If You can come down from the cross, we will believe You are the Messiah and sent by God. If You can't, we will know that You are a fraud and *cursed* by God."

It is one thing to be physically tortured to death, but to laugh and jeer at the one suffering is deplorable! Who can make fun of a man in misery? What kind of person does that? Yet during it all, Jesus had a God-like bearing. *Who is He? Can He possibly be who He claims to be?* A sign was hung above His head that read, "Jesus of Nazareth, King of the Jews." If this Jesus was being executed for insurrection and treason, why wasn't *that* also added?

Josh, on the other side of Jesus, joined in the jeering and said, "If You really are the Messiah, why don't You save Yourself—and us?"

I yelled at Josh, "Don't you fear God? You and I have been justly condemned and we are getting punished for our crimes. But this man, this Jesus, has done nothing wrong!"

I remembered again the things I had heard about Jesus. How He healed the sick, even raised a few people from the dead, and pardoned sin! *Pardon sin? Is that even possible for me? Isn't it too late for me? Can a dying man ask forgiveness from a dying man? Dare I ask?*

Finally, with my throat tight with emotion, I said, "Lord, remember me when You come into your kingdom."

Jesus turned His head toward me and with a voice full of compassion, said, "Truly I say to you, you will be with Me in paradise." With these words of forgiveness, a strange bright light came from Jesus' face. At that moment, all my pain was gone, and I had perfect peace and happiness. I was forgiven and accepted by God. Make no mistake, my severe physical suffering returned, but my mental anguish was gone. As long as Jesus and I were suffering together, I had peace.

Several women were among the crowd. They were crying and trying to comfort each other. One woman was supported by a young man. She looked severely grieved and brokenhearted. Pierced in her own heart. Jesus said to the young man, "Please take care of her." I assumed she was His own mother. The man immediately took her away from her heartbreaking scene. Then my thoughts went to my own mother. Would I want her here? After all the heartache I caused her, would she even come?

Darkness began to cover the land. The sun had previously been strong and bright. There developed a strange darkness everywhere. Then a darker cloud shrouded the cross of Jesus. Lightning occasionally flashed from that dark shroud. A hush fell over the unruly and vulgar mob. Some said God's curse was directed toward Jesus, "the Messiah impostor." Some ran!

Finally, when the dark gloom lifted, Jesus cried in a clear and trumpet-like voice, "It is finished." The sun broke through the heavy darkness and shone around the cross of Jesus. His face was bright as the sun as He looked toward heaven. He closed his eyes, bowed His head, and died. I was sorry He was gone but glad His suffering was over.

If these events weren't enough to convict the remaining rabble of their crimes against the innocent man hanging on the center cross, a violent earthquake now terrified them. Those who were most offensive in their jeering now had nothing to taunt. *I am sure this event will haunt them for the rest of their miserable lives!*

How has my life changed after meeting Jesus? Absolutely, it is the difference between heaven and hell. Jesus is dead now, but I know He will not forget me. As He promised, I will someday see Him again, in paradise. I don't know how much longer I will hang on this Roman implement of torture and execution and suffer this pain, but I have a bright future. I am no longer afraid of what any man or Roman can do to me. Praise God.

John

John the Beloved (One of the Twelve)

My name is John. I was originally a disciple of John the Baptist—"The voice crying in the wilderness." After Jesus was baptized at the Jordan River, John told Andrew and me to follow Him, but He had left the area and we didn't know where He was. Sometime later, about a month or so, we saw Jesus again, and followed Him. Cautiously at first and at a distance, until He turned and asked us, "What are you looking for?" A little timid, but determined, we said we wanted to be with Him and learn from Him. With a little nod and a great smile, we felt welcomed in His company.

While walking along, Jesus invited others to join Him too, including my brother James. We weren't exactly sure *who* this Jesus of Nazareth was, but we felt sure He was sent from God. Perhaps a wise rabbi? Perhaps a prophet? Could He be the Messiah, the Lamb of God, as John had said after His baptism?

We joined Jesus at a wedding feast in Cana, not far from Nazareth. After a few days, one of the servants was very upset that the wedding party had run out of wine. I saw Jesus' mother speak something privately to Him, then she told the servants to do anything Jesus told them to do. *What is going on? What did Jesus say to the servant? Why is he filling those large pots with water? And why is the servant tasting the water and taking some to the host? Water? Will they be serving water instead of wine?*

The water had miraculously turned to wine, and not the same quality as the first, but far superior. Upon tasting the new wine, everyone at the feast was amazed. This caused questions and aroused excitement from the bridegroom as well as the guests. When it was revealed that Jesus had changed the water to wine, everyone looked for Him. But He had quietly slipped away.

I was the youngest disciple and tried always to be as close to Jesus as possible. My hot temper, however, sometimes revealed my weakness and immaturity. I was too quick to criticize. Whenever I saw an injustice or an assault toward Jesus, I wanted to even the score. Take revenge! Carry out justice! My brother, James, and I were proud of being called the Sons of Thunder. We could be champions for Jesus, and strike whenever needed. One time, when Jesus was rudely treated by the Samaritans, we asked, "Master, may we call fire down from heaven to destroy these people?"

His response was, "You don't understand the spirit that is in you. I didn't come to destroy men, but to save them." I really didn't understand His passive manner!

He often talked about the kingdom of heaven. I didn't comprehend this kingdom of heaven, especially if He were to sit on David's throne and deliver Israel from the bonds of Rome. If only James and I could *prove* our love and loyalty to Jesus by resisting and taking up arms *against* the cruel government.

Slowly, ever so slowly, in observing the loving manner in which Jesus treated people, I saw in myself an evilness, an ugly temper, a vicious attitude. I truly wanted to be more like the Master! *Is that possible? Possible for one of the Sons of Thunder?*

Still, at every opportunity, James and I looked for openings to be as close to Jesus as possible. Our mother, bless her heart, was a follower of Jesus too and often served Him by offering whatever she could with her time and means. She, of course, wanted the best for her sons, which prompted her to ask Jesus for honored positions for James and me in the new kingdom. Jesus' answer was a question to *us*. In His mysterious *answer*, He asked if we were willing to drink of His cup, to stand trials and suffering for Him. That was not what we were asking, but still both of us said, "Yes, we are willing!"

Putting His hands on our shoulders, He said, "You will *indeed* do all that I have asked, but the honor of sitting beside Me on my throne is not of My choice, it is the Father's."

During my travels with Jesus, I saw many wonderful miracles. I never tired of seeing Jesus tenderly touch, heal, minister to the hungry and needy, and even raise the dead! He was becoming so popular that crowds pressed on Him from all sides. Even the Pharisees, who were constantly questioning and trying to trick Him, followed.

At the Passover in an upper room, all was set and ready except for a servant to wash our feet. James and I wanted to sit next to Jesus, one on each side. I am ashamed to say that there was a little shoving and pushing on my part. But Judas got the first seat to Jesus' left. I got the one on His right.

After everyone was settled, there was an uncomfortable silence. It was quiet, but not peaceful. It was soundless with eyes darting or downcast. *Where is the servant to wash our dusty feet? The basin and towel are here, but where is the servant? Do we wait for him? How long?* No one wanted to do the "honors," the humiliating undertaking of getting on our knees before our friends. That was the duty of a *servant!* Someone of lesser status, of lower class. Certainly not someone desiring to be sitting close to the king in the new kingdom.The silence was deafening and speaking to everyone in the room.

Finally, Jesus got up, walked to the basin of water and took the towel off the peg. He went directly to Judas and washed his feet first. It was hard to read the face of Judas. Was he pleased? Embarrassed? Uncomfortable? No one spoke during this foot-washing experience, except Peter. Peter, bless his heart, *first* refused to let Jesus wash his feet. Then requested his whole body be washed. Jesus was so gentle and kind to Peter, as He was with all of us. Finally, it was my turn. I was last, but I didn't care. Just the thought of this man, whom I believed to be the Son of God, loving me this much to take on the role of a servant and washing *my* feet, nearly broke my heart.

During the supper, Jesus became visibly troubled which was disturbing to the rest of us. I felt an evilness and a premonition of doom. Then our Master said that one of us was going to betray Him. *Betray Him? Never! I will fight for Him! I will die for Him!* Each man asked. "Lord, is it I?" Jesus remained silent. I searched my own heart and motives and then leaning closer, I whispered, "Lord, who is it?"

Then quietly, and for my ears only, Jesus said, "The one who dips his bread with Me is My betrayer." It was Judas! *Surely not Judas! He has the respect of all in this room. He is highly educated and well spoken. He holds the purse. He is sitting next to my Lord! Surely not! Not Judas!*

Finally, Judas asked, "Master, is it I?"

"You said correctly," Was Jesus' reply. At that Judas stood up. Then Jesus added, "Do quickly what you are planning to do." And Judas left! Still, it was not fully understood what had just happened. Did Jesus have an errand for Judas?

After the Passover supper, we went with Jesus to the Olive Garden where He often went to pray. While walking there, we needed to support His staggering steps. For some reason, He seemed fatigued, exhausted, and now silent. Upon entering the garden, Jesus asked us to pray. "Pray to keep from evil and from Satan's snares."

Yes, I prayed. And yes, I was sleepy, very sleepy! The previous hours had been emotional and stressful, and the hour was late. And yes, I slept! Slept soundly!

After about an hour, Jesus woke us up and asked why we couldn't pray for at least one hour. I remembered the promise I had made that I would drink from His cup, endure trials, and suffer with Him. *What is the matter with me? Why am I so weak? Is this my betrayal?* Again, He asked us to pray with Him. And again, my eyes were heavy and I slept! A strange and hypnotic stupor!

After another little while, Jesus was standing beside us as we heard the noise of a crowd coming toward us. In the lights of the flares, I saw Judas leading the mob, the temple guards, and Roman soldiers. In mock sympathy for Jesus, Judas ran up to Him and kissed Him.

Jesus was calm, poised, and like a mighty oak tree, He asked the mob, "Who are you looking for?"

"Jesus of Nazareth!"

"I am Jesus of Nazareth. I am the One you want, so let these men leave." In my weakness and in my fear of trials and suffering, I ran with the others. I ran like a weakling! I ran like a coward! If I had prayed like Jesus asked me to, would I have been strong enough to stand beside Him in His trials? I was so ashamed!

Convicted of my shame, I turned around and followed the mob at a safe distance, to see where they were taking my Lord. They roughly abused Him while walking back to the city. Jesus was taken first to the palace of the ex-high priest, Annas, for a preliminary questioning and accusing. Second, He was taken to the high priest palace, a Sadducee named Caiaphas. It was well after midnight, but the judgment hall was filled with Pharisees, rulers, judges, and Roman soldiers. At this point, I was determined to support Jesus. I did not conceal the fact that I was one of His disciples. I stayed on the sidelines, but as close to Jesus as possible. I was ready to testify on His behalf , but I was never asked.

False accusations were made. False allegations! Conflicting testimonies! And during it all, Jesus was calm and dignified—a striking contrast to His accusers who were angry, foulmouthed, frustrated, erratic, and volatile!

The Sanhedrin wanted and voted for Jesus' death, but they had no authority, under Roman rule, to execute *anyone*. Therefore, they needed some accusation they could bring to Pilate that would satisfy their corrupt desires. With weak allegations, they rushed Jesus to Pilate for his stamp of approval, which they were sure they could obtain. Pilate had been known to send innocent men to their deaths just to keep the peace with the powerful Jewish leaders.

Jesus was brought into Pilate's judgment hall to be questioned, but the Pharisees would not enter the hall because this was Holy Passover Week. They requested that the trial be held in the courtyard so they would not be "defiled" and denied participation in the Passover. No, they would not enter the hall, but they would accuse and demand the death of the Messiah, the *true* Passover Lamb.

When the leaders accused Jesus of stirring up discontent from Galilee to Jerusalem and talked about setting up a kingdom of His own, Pilate saw his opportunity to shift the responsibility to Herod Antipas, who was the ruler and king of this province, and currently in Jerusalem. I followed Jesus and the mob to Herod's judgment hall. Herod was furious and red-faced when Jesus refused to answer his questions or perform some miracle for him. I feared for Jesus' life when severe cruelty and barbarity were inflicted upon Him. In Herod's rage, he draped a dirty purple robe on Jesus' shoulders and sent Him back to Pilate.

The second trial by Pilate was only a pretense of justice. I was sure it would end in His death by Roman edict. I didn't stay any longer as I needed to tell Mary, Jesus' mother, what was happening... *This will break her heart. Do I dare bring her here? Can a mother, any mother, witness such cruelty? What will this do to the promise of her Son sitting on David's throne? What will it do to the rest of us—our hopes, our dreams of breaking the hated Roman power and control?*

By the time Mary and I got to Golgotha, the iron spikes were being driven into the precious hands and feet of Jesus. I was sorry I had brought Mary here and tried to encourage her to leave. But she wouldn't! With tears running down both of our faces, we remained at the cruel cross which bore the Son of God. Her body trembled with despair and helplessness.

Upon seeing His mother, Jesus said to her, "Mother, there is your son." And to me, He said, "Here now is your mother." At that statement, Mary was willing to leave the dreadful scene. I took her to my home.

A couple of days later, while some of the other disciples and I were mourning the loss of our Master, Mary Magdalene came running to us and cried, "Someone has taken the body of Jesus, and I don't know where. The tomb is empty!"

Peter and I ran out the door—the oldest and the youngest. I, of course, got to the tomb first and found it as Mary had described. The Roman soldiers were gone! The seal was broken! The tomb was empty! *Wasn't His death enough? Did they have to remove His body and defile it further?*

Wild stories were flying everywhere! Some said the Pharisees were claiming that we (Jesus' disciples), had gone during the night and had *stolen* His body. A few women who had gone to the tomb early that morning, said that two angels told them that Jesus was *alive!* Mary Magdalene returned, saying that this time she *saw* and *talked* to Jesus. A couple of men claimed they *saw* and *ate* with Jesus that day. All Peter and I saw was an empty tomb! Could it be true? *Can Jesus be alive?*

That evening, while in the upper room, there was much discussing and arguing among ourselves. Then Jesus appeared! Through closed and barred doors, He appeared! Terror changed to rejoicing in that hiding place. We had our Jesus, our Christ, our Messiah with us again.

We saw Jesus many times in the next several weeks. Before He ascended into heaven, He commissioned us to give the Good News to all the world and to make all nations His disciples. He promised He would be with us always, even to the end of the earth.

Has my life changed as a result of knowing Jesus? Changing from a hot-tempered and threatening attitude has been through the help of Jesus

Christ and the Holy Spirit. I am a very old man now and have suffered many trials and imprisonments, which I gladly bear for the name of Jesus Christ. I still long to sit beside Jesus on His throne because He has promised, "To him who is victorious, I will grant a place on My throne, as I myself was victorious and sat down with My Father on His throne." (Rev. 3:21, NEB)

CPSIA information can be obtained at www.ICGtesting.com
Printed in the USA
BVOW06s0012020916

460740BV00005B/12/P

9 781683 190875